"Don't wo~~rry, I won't be~~ putting you in one of the fishing shacks," John assured Dana.

"I told you about the fishing camp's grand opening tomorrow," he continued. "This is where we'll house our guests, right by the pond. I'm living here, so they'll always have someone handy if they need anything."

She twisted in the rocker, eyed the pond and the row of cabins. "This is really lovely."

Her compliment was sincere, and he immediately felt a sense of pride in the Cutters' first tourist venture. Hopefully the dude ranch would also hit the mark. "Thanks. Reservations are already coming in."

"Well, your business plan for the dude ranch was impressive. I'm sure the one you did for the fishing camp was equally impressive."

Even in her tousled state, Dana Brooks exuded elegance, yet John found her oddly easy to talk to. He hadn't ever held much interest in "city girls." But right now, ultimate city girl Dana Brooks had his attention, that was for sure.

Books by Renee Andrews

Love Inspired

Her Valentine Family
Healing Autumn's Heart
Picture Perfect Family
Love Reunited
Heart of a Rancher

RENEE ANDREWS

spends a lot of time in the gym. No, she isn't working out. Her husband, a former all-American gymnast, co-owns ACE Cheer Company, an all-star cheerleading company. She is thankful the talented kids at the gym don't have a problem when she brings her laptop and writes while they sweat. When she isn't writing, she's typically traveling with her husband, bragging about their two sons or spoiling their bulldog.

Renee is a kidney donor and actively supports organ donation. She welcomes prayer requests and loves to hear from readers. Write to her at Renee@ReneeAndrews.com, visit her website at www.reneeandrews.com or check her out on Facebook or Twitter.

Heart of a Rancher

Renee Andrews

Love Inspired

Recycling programs
for this product may
not exist in your area.

™ LOVE INSPIRED BOOKS

ISBN-13: 978-0-373-87796-6

HEART OF A RANCHER

www.LoveInspiredBooks.com

Printed in U.S.A.

Don't urge me to leave you or to turn back from you.
Where you go I will go, and where you stay I will stay.
Your people will be my people and your God my God.
—*Ruth* 1:16

This novel is dedicated to my niece,
Blaire Catherine Brown,
my inspiration for John's niece, Abi.

Chapter One

"So, when is the city girl going to make an appearance?" Landon Cutter finished cleaning the stalls while John hauled another fifty-pound bag of sweet feed into the barn.

John's phone beeped before he had a chance to answer his brother. He stacked the bag on top of the others he'd already hauled in, then fished the cell from his pocket and read the text. "How about that, her plane just landed." He glanced down at his sweat-soaked shirt, work jeans and boots. "Man, I've got to take a shower before she gets here."

"You've got plenty of time. It'll take her a good hour or so to make it to Claremont from Birmingham. Plus, from what I hear, it takes a while to get luggage at the airport."

John wasn't certain Landon was all that keen on his bringing in someone as prominent as Dana Brooks to their farm. Landon figured she wouldn't grasp the concept and appeal of down-home Southern pride. The

Brooks family of Chicago rivaled the Trumps in money and influence, so John had also been surprised that the late Lawrence Brooks's daughter had seen merit in his business plan. In fact, John had sensed an undeniable appreciation in her texts and conversations. And if anyone could sell his dude ranch idea, it was Dana Brooks.

"She didn't fly into Birmingham. Her plane landed at the local airstrip in Stockville." John removed his work gloves, slapped them together and tossed them on a shelf in the tack room. "They've got a private jet. She should be here in half an hour."

Landon whistled. "A private jet. Isn't that something? And she's coming here to help you start a dude ranch in North Alabama?"

"Reckon I must have won her over with my unique idea and Southern charm." John's smile was instant, but he fought to maintain his confidence about the classy lady hopping on a plane to see the ranch firsthand. And she planned to stay for a month, until they got the place up and running. How would he entertain a Chicago socialite on a ranch for four weeks? "I'm going down to the fishing shack to clean up before she gets here."

"Fishing cabin," Landon corrected. "And you'd better get used to calling them cabins, or Georgiana is liable to have your hide."

"Right, my fishing *cabin*." John didn't know if he'd ever get used to the term. Landon's wife, Georgiana, had the idea to turn the old fishing shacks on their property into something more habitable that would appeal to those interested in an outdoor getaway to fish and relax. Cutter's Fish Camp had only been open a couple of weeks but was doing great, with regular weekend reservations for five out of six cabins. John was thrilled with the early success, but he still wanted to succeed with his own business plan, the one the bank had so quickly turned down. However, business magnate Dana Brooks had faith in his dude ranch idea…and in John.

He saddled his horse, Red, and started across the fields toward the stocked pond and the fishing shacks—*correction*—cabins. When Landon married Georgiana, John insisted that the two of them, along with Georgiana's seven-year-old daughter, Abi, live in the Cutter family home, a two-story log cabin at the center of the property. He, on the other hand, would live in one of the fishing shacks and therefore be nearby whenever a fishing camp guest needed anything. He liked the rustic, compact cabin and the seclusion the place provided from the outside world. True, guests surrounded him when the cabins were rented, but the majority of the time they kept to themselves and he had the perfect place to meditate on God and study for his business degree.

The cabins were multicolored, Georgiana's idea to paint them similar to Charleston's Rainbow Row. Being blind, Georgiana often discussed the appeal of color and how she remembered hues from before she lost her sight. Consequently, the cabins were painted with the favorite colors from her memories. John hoped the look would appeal to the city girl, Dana Brooks. His cabin was sage-green and the smallest of the lot. He'd stuck a couple of rockers in the front, and Abi had helped him put blooming plants in big pots on each cabin's porch, including his own. Riding closer, he took in the colorful cabins, the sky turning turquoise in the early afternoon, the green mountains, the brown water from the pond. The place looked like a postcard or an ad for the newest dude ranch, the *only* dude ranch, in Alabama.

Maybe the scene would impress Dana Brooks.

He dismounted, and Red moved to graze near the cabin, then John glanced toward the edge of the property, toward the dirt road entrance, and noticed a gaping hole in the fencing. Undoubtedly his oldest and most ornery cow, Gypsy, had once again decided to play nomad. She'd been escaping since she was a calf, hence her name; now at nearly sixteen, Gypsy was already a year past the age Charolais cattle typically lived, and she still managed to escape. But nowadays she often got confused, wandering out, then wandering right back in. John scanned the field, but didn't spot Gypsy. He had no idea whether she was out or in, but either way, he had to fix that fence before he lost more livestock. You couldn't very well have a dude ranch without horses and cattle.

John withdrew his cell and noted the time on the display. *4:00 p.m.* Ms. Brooks would be getting a rental car in Stockville. Maybe that'd take enough time for him to repair the fence and clean up before she arrived.

God, help her like this place, and help me make a good first impression.

Dana stepped onto the tarmac while her copilot, Ned, unloaded her bags. She'd only needed Mark, her pilot, and Ned for the trip, so Ned had assumed the duty of assisting her while Mark got everything in order for their flight back to Chicago.

She'd requested a vehicle that would blend with farm country, some type of SUV, and the sole Stockville car rental agency had delivered nicely. A tall, thin man in a black T-shirt and blue jeans stood beside a white Cadillac Escalade parked nearby. Definitely not standard car-rental-agent attire, but he did have a name tag stating that he was Jesse Burger with Stockville Car Rental.

"Ms. Brooks." He moved quickly toward her with a way-too-broad smile in place. She wished people wouldn't get so nervous around her, but that was part of being the late Lawrence Brooks's daughter that she couldn't change.

The late Lawrence Brooks. Dana frowned, still having a difficult time getting used to the fact that her father was gone.

"I'm Jesse Burger." The friendly man grabbed her outstretched hand and pumped it vigorously.

"Nice to meet you, Jesse." She pushed her sadness aside and managed a smile for the friendly man.

"Welcome to Alabama. I hope you like your vehicle. We don't typically keep this type of SUV at the agency in Stockville, but we brought this one in from Birmingham just for you. I reckon you'll enjoy the ride. It's really sweet."

Reckon? Sweet? She was charmed by the accent and by the local flavor in his speech. It reminded her of the thick drawl she'd heard on the other end of the line the few times she'd spoken to John Cutter. "I'm sure it will be fine."

"I'll admit I kind of volunteered to go pick it up so I could drive it. I've never been in a Cadillac. Talk about a smooth ride. And it sits high on the road, almost as high as my dually." He motioned toward an oversize red pickup truck with two full doors and humongous tires, similar to those she'd seen in advertisements when the monster trucks were at the Sears Centre Arena in Chicago. Naturally, she'd never seen one of the big trucks up close. She was more of an opera and ballet kind of girl, but she couldn't deny that she found the oversize truck interesting. However, anxious to get to the Cutter ranch, she wouldn't take time for a perusal now.

"I went ahead and programmed that address where you said you were headed into the GPS. It's got all the roads already highlighted for you and ready to go. But really, you just take the main road from Stockville to Claremont. It's called Old Claremont Road if you're headed from here to there. If you're coming the other direction, it's Old Stockville Road."

"Seriously?" She'd never heard of anything so bizarre.

"Sure. Wouldn't make sense to give credit to only one of the towns." He grinned big.

"No, I guess it wouldn't." This trip was definitely going to be interesting. A road with two names, depending on which way you were driving. Her brother would never believe it.

"And that farm you're looking for is about dead center halfway. Shouldn't take you more than twenty minutes from here, I'd guess. Maybe fifteen, even."

"Thank you." She eyed the SUV. "I've never been

in anything like this, but I'm looking forward to it."
She had a Prius and a BMW in the garage, but hardly
ever went anywhere on her own. She'd wanted the en-
vironmentally friendly Prius but also hadn't been able
to resist the cute little red Z4. But even though she had
the two vehicles, a driver typically took her wherever
she wanted to go in Chicago. Driving amid paparazzi
had never been appealing, and they crowded her car
so terribly when she went to town that she'd practically forgone the fun of driving. She was rather excited
about the Escalade, and about the fact that the paparazzi
hadn't followed her on this venture. No sign of a camera anywhere.

Ned put the last of her bags in the back of the SUV.
"Ms. Brooks, will you need anything else before we
return home?"

"No, Ned. And I'll keep you posted on when I plan
to return. Should be four weeks or so." She was determined to show her brother, Ryan, that she could help
"young dreamers," as he called them, to make it in business. Their father had once been a young dreamer, and
he'd regretted not helping others do the same before
he died. Dana was doing this for him…and for herself.
She wanted to do the right thing, wanted to help others,
even if she had virtually no experience *yet*.

Her father's repeated words over the last few weeks
of his life echoed through her thoughts.

*"I was selfish. I forgot God, forgot myself. Only
cared about the money. More money. More power."*
Tears had slid down his weathered cheeks and pierced

Dana's heart. It'd been the first time she'd ever seen him cry. *"Don't end up like me, Dana."*

She'd vowed to him that she would follow his wishes. Now if she could get Ryan to understand that their father did have a change of heart before he died, that he really did encourage her to use funds from Brooks International to help rags-to-riches hopefuls.

Her cell phone rang, and her brother's name displayed, as if he were reading her very thoughts. She answered and put the phone on speaker while she climbed in the comfy SUV. "Hey, Ryan, give me a moment. I'm getting in my vehicle."

"Sure thing."

"There's heated seats." Jesse pointed inside the car. "Just push that button right there. But be careful, I tried 'em, and they get mighty hot mighty quick." He slapped the back of his jeans with a grin. "And all your payments and paperwork and everything were all taken care of. I guess you knew that. There's a copy of everything in your glove box. Oh, hang on, nearly forgot." He pulled a paper out of his back pocket. "I do need your signature on the contract showing the vehicle is okay and for the insurance and all."

"Thanks, Jesse." She signed the paper and closed the door.

"Heated seats." Ryan couldn't hold back his laugh. "Wow."

"He's a very sweet man." Dana watched Jesse Burger head toward his monster truck. "Very down-to-earth."

"I'll say. So, you already growing accustomed to Nowhere, Alabama?"

"I'm still at the airport, if you can call it that. I wouldn't say I'm accustomed yet, but it looks nice." She took in her surroundings, mountains in the distance, trees and fields all around. The airport was more of a runway in the middle of a pasture.

Jesse waved before climbing in his big truck, and Dana waved back.

"Nice. Right. Well, while you're hanging out with the farmers, I'll keep running the business in the real world." He paused, and she knew what was coming before he started. "Honestly, Dana, this is not what Dad wanted. Think of all the medications he was taking when he talked to you those last days. That wasn't our father. Do you seriously think he'd want you to turn your back on Brooks International? He built this company from the ground up, and he expected us to run it after he was gone. This business was his life."

"Exactly." Those were her father's precise words, in fact. "And he wanted more. He wanted to do more, help more, specifically help others more."

"Listen, I haven't got time to argue with you about it now. I've got a meeting with marketing in five minutes." He huffed out an exasperated breath. "I could use you here, Dana. That's your expertise, not mine."

"You said you had no problem with my giving this a try. And it *is* what Dad wanted, whether you believe it or not."

He ignored the last part of her statement. "For one month max. You promised me that."

"Right." She wished she hadn't agreed to a time limit on her act of goodwill. What if it took longer than a

month to get a dude ranch up and running in North Alabama? Her dad had wanted to help others, and John
Cutter had impressed her immensely on the college
entrepreneurial forum she'd joined online. Plus, she'd
been drawn to the country drawl, the enthusiasm for
his business plan and the optimism that radiated from
the Alabama rancher. In fact, she couldn't wait to meet
the guy. "I've got to go, Ryan. I'll call you in the morning and let you know how things are going."

"Fine," he muttered before disconnecting.

Starting the SUV, Dana glanced at the GPS and
began her drive to the farm, thinking about the cowboy with the delicious Southern drawl. Did he look as
good as he sounded on the phone? She'd searched the
internet for John Cutter, of course, but there was no
sign of a Facebook page or anything else with a photo
on it. No, she couldn't see herself with a country boy
long-term, but John Cutter did have *something*. His
texts were witty, their conversations interesting, and
she found herself a little nervous about meeting the Alabama rancher. Dana couldn't remember the last time
she'd been nervous about, well, anything.

Her suitcases bumped against each other when she
turned out of the airport, and she wondered if she'd even
brought the right clothing for this trip. She had an entire
suitcase for shoes. Right now she wore typical travel-
wear, a navy-and-white jacquard cardigan over a matching shell, a navy gabardine skirt and high-heel pumps.
Granted, she wanted to impress him with her business
panache, but she also had to admit that she had no idea
about appropriate ranchwear. She planned to head out

shopping as soon as she got the right attire in mind, because while she did want him to see her as a businesswoman, she also wanted him to see her as approachable. Maybe even very approachable. She'd heard Southern men were gentlemen and treated ladies "right."

Every guy she dated in Chicago seemed to be after the Brooks name and money. John Cutter didn't come across that way. He came across as black and white, honest to a fault, particularly when he told her all the reasons the bank gave for turning down his business plan. No genuine investor would ever fund a dude ranch in the middle of who-knows-where, Alabama.

But she would.

The GPS showed she was eighteen minutes from her destination, twenty-five minutes with traffic. An empty road stretched ahead, fields along both sides, mountains in the distance. Not a single car to be seen. "Eighteen minutes it is."

Eager to begin this journey—and meet John Cutter— Dana pressed her foot on the gas and increased her speed. She was surprised at how much she looked forward to meeting the cowboy with the big dreams and the strong faith. He'd mentioned God and family in nearly every phone call. Her father had finally found faith near the end. Dana didn't plan to wait that long, and she suspected that John Cutter might be the right person to show her...

Her thoughts were cut short when she rounded the curve and came face-to-face with two dark eyes in a white hairy face. Slamming on the brakes, she attempted to turn the wheel, but the next thing she knew the cow had dropped, and smoke billowed from under the hood.

"Oh no, oh no, oh no!" Dana jumped out of the Escalade and surveyed the damage. Front end bashed in, and big white cow, motionless on the ground. "Oh, what have I done!" She ran back to the driver's seat and grabbed her purse, yanked out her cell and, with hands trembling, dialed Ryan.

No signal flashed back from the display.

She'd never in her life been unable to get a cell signal. "No way, no way." Trees surrounded the road and stretched as far as she could see in both directions. She'd been in the curvy stretch of road for quite some time and couldn't remember seeing any houses. How long had she been driving? Surely she wasn't that far from the Cutter farm. "Okay, Brooks, you can do this." Sliding her purse strap over her shoulder, she began the walk ahead while trying her very best not to take another look at the large, white, undeniably dead animal in the middle of the road. "I'm so sorry," she whispered as she passed. For all she knew, she'd killed someone's pet.

She peered ahead, didn't spot any sign of civilization and realized she'd never felt so alone. "God, please, help me get there safely." Prayer still felt a little foreign on her lips, but she planned to work on that, starting now. She'd killed a cow and had virtually no idea where she was.

Definitely a time for higher guidance.

The walk started easily, and she was glad her Christian Louboutin pumps were so comfortable. However, the "paved" road was pitifully surfaced, and by the time she'd gone fifteen minutes, even the Louboutins were feeling a bit defeated. She was certain some of those pointed rocks had pushed through her soles. A trickle of perspiration edged down her spine, as well as along her forehead. She unbuttoned the cardigan and thought about taking it off, then she noticed that she actually had a sweat line on her shell. Sure, she liked to sweat in a gym with her personal trainer, but she didn't want to be drenched the first time she met John Cutter.

"Hit a cow, wreck a truck and walk a mile. Welcome to Alabama," she said, finally spotting a break in the trees ahead. In spite of her aching feet, Dana picked up her pace and hurried to the gravel side road. An oversize aluminum mailbox at the end had Sanders painted in white on the side, as did a big wooden arch that hovered over the apparent driveway. She looked down the length of the gravel and couldn't spot the end. There was a farm down there, no doubt, but it wasn't close. And it didn't belong to John Cutter.

Walk the driveway and hope to find help, or keep going and find the Cutter farm? Assuming one farm probably led to another, she kept walking. Ten minutes later she saw the next opening in the trees, this one with a dirt road and the name Cutter on the equally large silver mailbox, as well as burned into the wooden arch that showcased the driveway. A new sign had been added under the center of the arch that read Cutter's Fish Camp—Guests Welcome.

He had told her about the business venture that the bank had approved, and Dana looked forward to seeing a "fish camp" in action. But right now she mainly looked forward to finding the house, briefly meeting the cowboy—she didn't want to spend too much time with him before she had a nice, long shower—and getting to her hotel so she could freshen up. Oh, and letting someone know she'd left a dead SUV and a dead cow in the road on the way to the farm.

That probably wasn't the best form of an introduction. But, unfortunately, that's all she had.

She started down the driveway but didn't make it far before she heard a loud pounding and a lot of grunting. Slowing her steps, she approached the cowboy apparently stretching wire across the fence. A black Stetson covered the top of his face, and sweat visibly dripped from his chin to the ground as he worked. He was, in a word, quite beautiful.

Dana's throat grew dry. He wore a navy T-shirt that showcased broad shoulders, notable biceps and abs that would impress any personal trainer. His jeans had that well-worn look, displaying his long legs. At least six feet tall, possibly six-one or six-two. She certainly never saw guys who looked like that in Chicago. And if this was a hired hand, she had to wonder what the ranch owner looked like. She cautiously stepped toward the working cowboy, and when he only grunted and pulled the wire some more, she took a few more steps closer and cleared her throat.

He stopped midgrunt, looked up and treated her to the most exquisite pair of amber eyes she'd ever seen. Almost gold, and squinting in the late-afternoon sun.

He grinned, straight white teeth amid a perfectly

tanned face. Goodness, she should've found a reason to visit Alabama years ago.

"Kind of overdressed there, aren't ya?"

She thought she recognized the voice, but she wasn't certain. Did all guys down here sound that way? Or was this the rancher she'd been talking to for weeks? Only one way to find out. "I'm looking for John Cutter."

His grin broadened, the two deep dimples creasing his cheeks somehow managing to make him look even better. "Well, Ms. Brooks, you've found him."

Dana's pulse quickened. Have mercy, his looks matched the voice. John Cutter was real, genuine, honest and gorgeous.

He lifted a brow, peered past her down the road then quirked his mouth to the side. "Where's your car? Did you break down? Are you okay?" He took a step toward her. "Hey, I can help you out."

Words weren't coming, and she'd never been one to be at a loss for words. But she'd also never been this close to a cowboy who looked as if he'd stepped off the front of a romance novel, standing there all muscled and sweaty from good, honest work, with the mountains in the distance and the fields full of horses and cattle behind him. Horses and white cattle. White cattle that looked…oddly familiar.

Suddenly the words came, and she wished she had thought a moment before blurting them so clearly.

"Oh, no. I hit your cow!"

Chapter Two

With the fence taking longer than he'd expected, John figured Dana Brooks would show up before he finished, so he'd resolved himself that he'd be a sweaty mess when he met the classy lady. What he hadn't anticipated, however, was that she'd be a sweaty mess, too.

The silky blond hair he'd seen in so many photos online was now a combination of flat and frizzy at the same time. Her face had a perspiration glow, and her clothing was way over the top for farm attire. She looked like she did in those online photos, except she didn't look quite so put together. And she'd definitely had better days, because she'd just announced that she'd hit his cow. He didn't have to wonder which cow.

Removing his gloves, he wiped the sweat from his forehead with the back of his sleeve then, glad the repair was done, stuck his pliers in his back pocket. "I'm guessing Gypsy is dead?"

"Gypsy?" Her eyes widened so much he could see white all the way around the vivid blue. "Oh, no, I killed your pet!" A hand flew to her mouth. "I'm so sorry." Her words were muffled behind her palm. Then she looked back toward the road. "Maybe, maybe she wasn't dead. Maybe she was just knocked out or something." She turned back to John with a slight look of hope.

He raised a brow, quirked his lip to the side. "Exactly what were you driving?"

"An Escalade."

He shook his head. "Probably not just knocked out."

Another whimper, and he found himself moving toward the pretty lady who'd killed his oldest cow. "Hey, come on, I'll get you a glass of water, and then we'll get everything taken care of." He opened the gate to let her in. "It'll be okay."

She trembled from head to toe, so he wrapped an arm around her as they moved toward his cabin, then he guided her to the nearest rocker on the porch. "Gypsy has been on her last leg for quite a while, and we were really just waiting for her time to go. She wasn't a pet—" he lifted a shoulder "—but we tend to get to know all our cattle."

"I am *so* sorry." She looked miserable, and she kept glancing back toward the road as though she half expected Gypsy to make a miraculous recovery and show up at the gate, ready to be let in.

John was fairly certain that wouldn't happen. "It'll be okay. I'll call my brother, Landon, and tell him what's happened. We'll get everything taken care of, and I'm gonna go get you that glass of water." He went inside and fixed two glasses of ice water, called Landon and gave him a heads-up on the situation then walked back out to find Lightning, his hound dog, sniffing Dana's expensive shoe. "All right, boy. She's had a bad enough afternoon already. Don't even think about it."

"Think about what?" Dana asked.

Lightning, only slightly younger than Gypsy, raised a droopy eye, moved to one of the porch rails and proceeded to do his business.

John nodded toward the dog.

Dana sputtered on her water with a little laugh. "Oh, I see."

"I'd kind of expected to welcome you to the ranch a little more appropriately." He took a long drink of water, the cool liquid hitting his parched throat like a balm, almost as refreshing as having a stunning woman sitting on his front porch. "Don't suppose hitting a cow and walking a mile in high heels would send you running to the hills, would it?"

Her eyes glittered above her glass and the corners of her mouth turned up as she took another sip. "As long as you don't want to banish me to the hills for killing your cow."

"As I said, Gypsy was probably ready to go. She may have even gone out to the road with a death wish, hoping someone would put her out of her misery." He took another drink of water. "Her arthritis was pretty bad."

She looked suspicious. "Are you serious?"

He grinned. "Nah, just trying to make you feel better."

She gave him a full smile, and he noticed she was even prettier when she smiled. "Well, it worked."

"Good." He finished off his water, nodded toward her nearly empty glass. "Want more?"

"No, thank you." She relaxed in the rocker and leaned her head back, her blond hair tumbling past slender shoulders.

John took in her appearance again. Even a sweaty mess, Dana Brooks made his pulse kick up a notch. She was taller than he'd imagined, merely a few inches shy of his six-two, and her eyes were bluer than the photos depicted. Her bio on the internet said she was twenty-six, two years younger than John, but she had a soft-ness to her complexion, a tenderness to her features, that made her appear even younger. But her eyes, those inquisitive Caribbean-blue eyes, appeared wiser than her years, studying everything around her as she sat on the porch.

In fact, while he studied her, she visibly took in her surroundings—the porch, his dog, the fields, grazing livestock and the other colorful cabins lined up along the pond's edge. Then she drew her attention back to John. "Is this where you live?"

He knew about her high-rise apartment in Chicago and how it overlooked Lake Michigan and the ritzy art district. "This is it. But don't worry, I'm not putting you in one of the fishing shacks." He cleared his throat. "Fishing cabins, I mean. Gotta get used to that."

She shook her head. "Oh, no, I didn't mean for your family to provide accommodations. I made a reserva-tion at a hotel in town."

"Yeah, but Georgiana, my brother's wife, said she wouldn't accept your staying in a tiny hotel room when you could stay out here on the farm. Plus, if you want to see the place firsthand, you might as well stay here." He grinned, thinking about Georgiana's insistence that their guest stay on the ranch. "There's only one hotel in town—I'm sure you figured that out. Or if you want to get specific, there aren't *any* hotels in town. We have one bed-and-breakfast, and that's it."

"Yes, the Claremont Bed-and-Breakfast. That's where I made my reservation."

"Naturally we know the owners, Mr. and Mrs. Tingle. So Georgiana gave them a call and told them you wouldn't need a place to stay, after all."

Her mouth opened slightly, surprise filling her expression. "She canceled my reservation?"

"Not exactly. I mean, they're waiting for you to call and officially cancel it, but she did tell them you'd be staying on the farm." He leaned against the porch rail.

Her hands ran up and down the length of her glass, ice cubes rattling with the movement, as she apparently accepted the way things ran in Smalltown, U.S.A. Quite the contrast from Chicago, no doubt. "I wouldn't want to be a burden."

He stopped short of laughing out loud. "You've already killed our oldest cow—can't get much more of a burden than that."

Her mouth fell completely open this time, and John set his laugh free. Then, seeing her shocked expression, he sobered as best he could.

"Sorry, I probably shouldn't tease you until you get to know me better. You aren't a burden—you're company. We tend to think a lot of our guests, and that's what you are. And you'll have to take it up with Georgiana if you're planning to turn down her offer. But trust me, she'll put up a decent fight. And I'm sure you can tackle the best of city slickers in a boardroom, but you haven't seen anything like Georgiana Cutter when she has her mind made up." He shrugged. "In my opinion, you should just go ahead and concede. I'm just sayin'."

Her hands stopped fidgeting with the glass, and she laughed. "I'll think about it." She leaned forward and took another look at the line of fishing shacks bordering one side of the pond. "So, is this where your dude ranch guests will stay? In these cabins?"

"No, our fishing camp guests stay here, so they can be right by the pond. Makes it easier for them to start fishing at the crack of dawn, when the bream and crappie bite best. I'm living in this one, so they'll have someone handy if they need anything. For the dude ranch, we'll have campsites by the creek that flows by the hiking trails. I'll show you when we tour the ranch."

She scanned the vast pond. Cattails bordered the ends and dark green lily pads dotted the banks with an occasional white lily balancing on top, the scene peaceful and still beneath the afternoon sky. "No one's fishing," she said. "You don't have any guests here now?"

"Nah, it's barely March. Fish don't start biting much until nearly April, so right now we only have guests on the weekends. Most of them are here more to relax than because they're die-hard fishermen. But reservations are already picking up for next month."

"So you have some guests coming in tomorrow, on Saturday?"

"All cabins filled but mine."

She twisted in the rocker, eyed the pond and the colorful row of cabins. "This is really lovely."

Her compliment was sincere, and he immediately felt a sense of pride in the Cutters' first tourist venture. Hopefully the dude ranch would also hit the mark. "Thanks. We're fairly excited about the rentals and reservations."

"Well, your business plan for the dude ranch was impressive. I'm sure the one you did for the fishing camp was, too."

John had prepared the business plan for the camp, but it was Georgiana's brainstorm, not his. "Yeah, the bank had no problem with the fishing camp. But they had no desire to fund the dude ranch."

"Well, I think it's a great idea, and I'm excited that Brooks International is funding the project."

"Trust me, I'm very glad about that." He reached for her glass, and she handed it over, her lean fingers brushing his palm in the process. It could have been John's imagination, but it appeared her cheeks flushed a little when their hands touched.

Even in her tousled state, she exuded elegance, yet John found her oddly easy to talk to. He hadn't ever had much interest in "city girls," especially after MaciJo Riley left his heart in her wake when she chased after her big-city dreams. But right now, this city girl had his attention—that was for sure.

Her throat pulsed as she swallowed. "So did you call your brother?"

"I did. He's waiting for us to head up to the main

house so he and I can go check on your accident. We'll get the rental agency to tow the Escalade and we'll take care of Gypsy."

She straightened in the rocker. "Take care of Gypsy?"

"Yes." He didn't elaborate.

Evidently she understood that she didn't want to hear how they would go about taking care of a dead cow. She merely nodded. "And we're going to the main house now?"

"If you're up to it."

She stood, looked around the front of the cabin and then toward Red, still grazing nearby. The log cabin was a good piece away, and naturally she couldn't see it from there. Nor could she see a vehicle, he realized, since John didn't need one at the shack.

"How are we getting to the main house?" The tiny tremor of trepidation in her tone made him fight another smile.

"I rode Red down here, but I thought we'd take the Gator back, given that your skirt isn't exactly conducive to horse riding." He watched Lightning take another interest in her shoes, and he gently steered the old dog in the other direction.

She didn't notice the dog, her attention more focused on his statement. "The gator?"

John loved how she attempted to sound calm when her eyes gave her away. What, did she think he had some sort of live alligator around that they'd ride to the big house? He might live in the sticks, but he wasn't ready to be featured on *Swamp People* yet. He leaned down to scratch Lightning behind the ears and checked his grin. "Come on, I'll show you." Then he led her behind the cabin to the small work shed he'd recently added for fishing supplies, opened the rolling door and pointed to the John Deere Gator that he and Landon used around the fields when they weren't on horseback. "That's my Gator, and it's a decent ride. Probably not as fancy as your Escalade, but I can guarantee we won't hit any cows."

"*That's* your gator." Relief flooded through her words.

He climbed into the driver's seat, pointed to the passenger side. "Yep. You ready to go?"

She stood still for a moment, and John wondered if she expected him to usher her in. There wasn't a door to open; the thing was basically an oversize dune buggy. So, if she wasn't a princess waiting for a chauffeur to open her door, why was she standing there?

"Everything okay?" he asked.

"Yes, yes, it's fine." She blinked, took a step toward the Gator, and then he saw her dilemma—how to get in wearing that skirt. But before he could offer suggestions, she attempted to climb in ladylike and did a pretty good job. The skirt was slim and fitted, so she sat on the seat and then gracefully moved both legs into the vehicle. Then she let out a relieved sigh. "I've never seen one of these before."

Impressed at her ability to adapt, John started the Gator. "They're pretty much a standard piece of equipment for farms around here."

She examined the bright yellow seats and the equally bright green exterior, then ran her hand across the shiny black dash. "It looks amazingly fun."

City girl or not, she was mighty cute. "You want to drive? It's fine with me, as long as you promise not to take out any more livestock on the way to the house."

She didn't mask her excitement with that prospect quickly enough, and John suspected—previous cow collision or not—she was about to hop out, round the Gator and take the wheel. But then she shook her head. "Not today, but yes, I'd like to drive it eventually." She sounded practically giddy over driving a Gator. And to think John had wondered if he'd be able to impress the Chicago debutante. "And I promise not to hit any more cows when I do," she added.

"I'll hold you to that." Grinning, he backed out of the shed. "So a future Gator drive will go on the books. I'm thinking we'll probably ride the acreage tomorrow so I can show you what I have in mind for the round pen, the campsites, trail rides and all. We can take the Gator for that, rather than ride horses."

"Oh, I want to ride horses, too." She paused, looked at Red, then at the other horses meandering nearby and the multitude of Charolais cattle grazing on the hill. "I need to try everything if I'm going to tell the Brooks International board everything about the ranch. I want this to work, so they'll agree to fund other similar projects."

"I want this to work, too." John noticed her slight smile and suspected she looked forward to her weeks on the farm. Again, a trickle of pride shot straight to his heart.

They passed over the fields with Dana surveying everything, her blond hair whipping wildly in the breeze. She gathered it into a makeshift ponytail and held it with one hand, while using the other to shield her eyes as she took everything in. She reminded him of Abi last fall at the county fair, absorbing all the new sights, sounds and fun. This affluent woman, a millionaire who'd already made her mark following after her father as a venture capitalist, seemed captivated by *his* world.

John was so busy watching her that he forgot to slow down when they approached the biggest hill in the pasture and consequently caught a bit of air. She grabbed at the dashboard before she slammed back down on the seat.

"Whoa!" Her excited laugh filled the air, and John found himself joining in.

"Sorry," he said, slowing down and deciding to take it easy for the remainder of the journey. No need to toss her into the field on her first day at the ranch.

She'd lost her grip on her hair when they went airborne, and it whipped in front of her eyes as her laughter subsided. He watched her gather it again and pull it away from her face, and the pale pink polish on her nails shimmered in the sun and added another extremely feminine quality to the woman riding next to him.

John pulled his attention away to make certain he didn't hit any more unexpected hills, and then he heard her gasp as the log cabin and barn came into view.

All of her attention focused on the scene. "Oh, my, it's beautiful!"

He'd always thought so, but he was a country boy, and this was pure country. Hearing her echo his sentiments with such enthusiasm, particularly when he wanted so much to impress her with the ranch, felt good.

"That's Abi." His niece, her strawberry pigtails bouncing as she jumped off the porch, ran toward the approaching Gator.

"Hey, Uncle John! Is that the city lady? Are you really from a big town where the wind blows all the time? Uncle John says you're going camping with us so you can see what it's like, 'cause when we have a dude ranch people will camp and hike and stuff. I haven't been camping before, but we're gonna be in a tent and cook hot dogs and marshmallows, and you eat everything with your fingers. But it's okay, 'cause you can lick your fingers to get the gooey stuff off when you're done."

John barely got the Gator turned off before Abi stood within feet of Dana. And continued asking questions.

"You sure are dressed up. Did you go to church? Today is Friday, not Sunday. Did we miss church?"

"Abi, this is Miss Dana." John hoped his niece would stop talking long enough for the introduction, and she obliged. "And no, we didn't miss church."

"These are the clothes I wore to work this morning, and then on the plane." Dana smiled at Abi, and John could see that she, like John and everyone else who met the precocious child, was smitten. "I didn't dress right for the farm, did I?"

"Nope, you sure didn't." Abi's head shook so hard her curly pigtails practically slapped her freckled cheeks. "You dressed for church. Or really, you kind of dressed for Easter or maybe Christmas, a fancy church day, not a regular church day."

John laughed, and Dana grinned.

"I did bring a couple of outfits that might work on the farm, but I'm pretty sure I'll need to go shopping and buy some more. Maybe you and your mommy could help me find a place to buy some farm clothes while I'm here?"

Abi's head shake turned to a full, enthusiastic bob. "Sure we can! I like to go shopping, and Mommy does, too. And Grandma comes sometimes. We can go to the square, and we can get candy at the Sweet Stop and then go to the toy store, and maybe we can go get a double-chocolate milk shake when we finish. I'll go tell Mommy. Are you ready to go?"

This time Dana laughed. "Well, I was thinking maybe tomorrow. I've kind of had a full day already today. And I do have some clothes I can wear, as soon as I get my bags from the car."

"We'll get those for you." John climbed out of the Gator.

"Oh, all right, then." Her disappointment undeniable, Abi handled it pretty well for a seven-year-old. "I guess tomorrow will be okay. But tomorrow is Saturday, so I have my riding lessons from Grandma in the morning. But we can go after that."

Dana didn't know when she'd seen a more adorable little girl. Abi's curly red hair, copper freckles and intriguing hazel eyes reminded her of the young actress who'd played Annie on Broadway. Except, in Dana's opinion, little Abi was even cuter, with a realness that could only be attributed to being raised on a ranch, surrounded by family and grounded in rural country. All foreign to Dana.

Abi's attire also set her apart from any little girl Dana had ever been around. She wore a yellow shirt with denim cutoff shorts and bare feet. Even when she'd been playing as a child, Dana never went without shoes. The feature only added to Abi's appeal; this was a true country girl. "Maybe I could come and watch your horseback-riding lessons." She hoped to add some consolation for making Abi wait until tomorrow to shop.

Freckled cheeks pumped up with her smile. "Okay!" Then she proceeded to tell Dana about everything she'd learned in her riding lessons, while the cabin door opened and another tall cowboy Dana knew must be John's brother stepped onto the porch. The exact image of John, except where John's light brown hair was wavy and a little longer, Landon had a short, military style. But they had the same broad grin, the same amber eyes and the same deep dimples bracketing their smiles. Definitely brothers.

"Abi, let her get a word in every now and then." He stepped off the porch and tweaked one of Abi's pigtails. "You'll have to learn to talk when she takes a breath. I'm Landon, and we're glad you're here, Ms. Brooks, even if you've gotten off to a rocky start with your arrival on the farm."

A rocky start. Right. With all her attention focused on John, she'd almost forgotten about her entrance to the ranch. "I'm so sorry about Gypsy." The guilt of killing this family's oldest cow hit her hard as she continued to meet more of the Cutters.

"Gypsy? Is Gypsy okay?" Abi's question caused Dana to realize that rarely being around children had removed her natural protective filter for the information she should share. Abi's attention moved to the field. "Where is Gypsy?"

"Um…" Dana looked to John for help.

His mouth shifted to the side as though debating what to say, but then the cabin door opened again and a woman stepped out. Her hair, the same strawberry-blond as Abi's, fell in long waves to her waist. "Abi, your chocolate milk is ready and on the kitchen table. Why don't you come on in and drink it while it's good and cold?"

"Yum." Abi scrambled past the group and hurried into the house.

Landon looked adoringly at the stunning woman. "Ms. Brooks, this is Georgiana, my wife."

"Please call me Dana." She already felt over-the-top formal in her business suit and didn't want them addressing her formally, as well. Looking back, she knew that wearing the outfit instead of something more casual was a mistake. It put a barrier up between her and this kind family, so willing to take her in and to forgive her for killing their cow.

"All right, then," Landon said, his Southern drawl stretching out the words. "Georgiana, this is Dana."

"Nice to meet you," Dana said.

"You, too." Georgiana lowered her voice and explained, "The window is open. I heard Abi's question about Gypsy and thought it'd be a good time for her to have her chocolate milk."

Landon wrapped an arm around his wife and kissed her cheek. "Smart thinking."

"I feel terrible about what happened." Dana sensed the warmth of John's presence before she turned to verify that he'd moved to her side.

"We live on a ranch with a lot of livestock. We're kind of used to the fact that they don't all live forever." His rich baritone sent goose bumps marching down her arms. Thank goodness for the long sleeves on her cardigan.

Dana had no idea how she'd control this crazy response to the cowboy. No guy from the city had ever had this effect on her senses, where every cell in her being seemed to stretch toward him whenever he neared. She knew she should say something, but once again, staring at those two dimples bracketing his smile, she found herself speechless.

Landon turned to John. "I talked to the guy at the rental car place in Stockville. They've got someone on their way to tow the vehicle, so we should go get Ms. Brooks's—Dana's—things out before they haul it."

"All right." John turned to Dana. "You good to stay here with Georgiana and Abi while we get your luggage?"

Thankfully, her brain started working again, and she found words. "Sure."

"They're getting you another vehicle, but it won't be delivered until tomorrow afternoon. That okay?" Landon asked. "You can use one of ours in the meantime if you need to go anywhere. But you should know that Georgiana already canceled your room at the bed-and-breakfast. We want you to stay here."

"Technically it isn't canceled, but I told the Tingles that we planned on your staying at the ranch, unless you'd rather not," Georgiana said. "But I can't imagine you'd enjoy being in a tiny room cooped up over the next few weeks. Out here you can have run of the place and the land. Plus, you'll be able to visit the farm firsthand every day, be around the horses. And you've probably already figured out how much we love having company."

"That's fine." Dana was surprised that the family so easily took her in, working her into the day effortlessly. "I appreciate all your help."

"Not a problem at all." Georgiana's smile claimed her face, and Dana was taken aback by her natural beauty. Hazel eyes in a heart-shaped face, copper freckles, bright smile. In a green T-shirt, denim capris and bare feet, she looked as pretty as any model.

"Georgiana, Dana isn't exactly dressed for the farm, and since we might be gone a little while, do you think you could get her something more comfortable to wear?" John asked, then added, "Right now, she's wearing a suit and heels."

Dana wondered why John described what she wore, since Georgiana looked directly at her, and then the pieces clicked into place. The beautiful woman was blind.

"Oh, my, you broke down and had to walk all that way in a suit?" Georgiana asked. "Bless your heart. Yes, come on in, and we'll find you something to wear. Abi can help. She loves picking out clothes. She helps me all the time." Georgiana laughed. "It's kind of hard for me to match things, you know."

"Georgiana will take care of you until we get back." John's voice was quiet, and Dana turned to see that his eyes held an admiration and kindness toward his sister-in-law. He was right; regardless of her disability, Georgiana wanted to take care of her guest, and Dana wanted to let her.

"That's fine," she turned to Georgiana. "I'd love to borrow something, if you don't mind. And I'll call the bed-and-breakfast and let them know I'm officially canceling my reservation."

Georgiana clasped her hands together. "Wonderful. We're so glad you'll be staying with us."

"One thing, though, Georgiana," Landon said.

"What's that?"

"She's got a good four or five inches of height on you. Probably want to consider that when you're finding her clothes."

Georgiana's grin showcased the copper freckles on her cheeks and the hazel in her eyes. "So if she wears my pants, we're talking high waters." She lifted a shoulder. "Not a problem. I hear capris are in this year." She waved a hand toward her own outfit.

Dana already liked the woman. "You heard right. They definitely are."

"We'll have dinner ready when y'all get back so John can eat before he heads to work," Georgiana said to the rugged cowboys walking toward an old blue truck, their boots kicking up a bit of dust as they moved.

"Sounds great." John climbed into the passenger side of the old pickup, looked at Dana and knuckled his Stetson. "Oh, by the way, welcome to the ranch."

She stood beside Georgiana and watched them drive away, mesmerized with the lifestyle so different than her own. And equally mesmerized by the breathtaking cowboy with the sexy smile, and eyes that looked like honey in the sunshine.

"Come on, we'll go get you some clothes." Georgiana took a couple of steps, opened the door and led the way inside. If Dana didn't know she was blind, she wouldn't have been able to tell.

They entered the log cabin, and Dana viewed the beauty of plank wood ceilings, hardwood floors, exposed beams and a huge stone fireplace. Even the furnishings were rustic but homey. "Your room is upstairs, on the left. I'll show you." Georgiana started up the stairs. "Abi, you can come help me pick out some of my clothes for Miss Dana to wear if you're done with your milk."

"Cool!" Abi abandoned her spot at the kitchen table and ran toward the stairs.

"I didn't hear you put your glass in the sink." Georgiana's motherly tone was endearing.

"Oh, yeah, right." Abi turned, ran back to the table and moved her empty glass to the sink. Then she darted back across the living area to pass them going up the stairs. "I'll go pick out something nice."

Georgiana laughed. "Abi loves to help." She slid her hand along the wall until it met the first door facing and then pointed to the open door. "That's your room. There is an adjoining bathroom, and you should have all the linens and things you need, but if anything is missing, just let me know. We really are glad you're here."

Dana peeked in. A multicolored quilt covered the bed and another hung over a quilt rack near the window. Antique furniture filled the room with crocheted doilies accenting each piece. "The quilts and the doilies are lovely."

"Mrs. Cutter made those before she passed on. When I was little and came over to ride horses with Landon, she was often on the front porch crocheting. I'm sure John will probably tell you, but they lost their mother eight years ago. She'd gotten depressed after her husband died in a farming accident and unfortunately turned to prescription meds. John was the one who found her. Landon was overseas serving in Afghanistan, and John became the man of the house here, taking care of the farm and their little brother, Casey."

Dana had known that John's parents were dead, but she hadn't realized the amount of responsibility he'd inherited. He'd mentioned Casey and the fact that he was at the University of Alabama, but he hadn't said anything about raising the boy after his mother died. "How old was Casey when she died?"

"I believe he was ten, maybe eleven." Georgiana leaned against the door frame. "John saw him through all those teenage years and all the trouble that typically comes with them. And Casey turned out well, even if they had a few bumps along the way."

"Mom, are y'all coming?" Abi's voice echoed down the hall.

"And speaking of kids…" Georgiana shook her head, turned and continued down the hall.

Touched by the hospitality from this family, Dana felt an even stronger desire to make certain John's dude ranch became a success after learning everything he'd gone through over the past few years.

As though she knew what Dana was thinking, Georgiana said, "John is really hoping this dude ranch idea will work, and he believes you're the one who can make it happen."

"It's a good idea." Dana believed it was, even if it wasn't one that any wise investors would fund. And why wouldn't they? Sure, Alabama wasn't a typical location for a dude ranch, but if she could market it well, there shouldn't be a problem. Then again, in the back of her mind she wondered if she had missed something. Was there more to getting an honest-to-goodness dude ranch up and running than she'd realized?

They entered Georgiana and Landon's room, where Abi had gathered a few tops and pants and tossed them on the bed.

"Do you like any of those?" Abi asked. "Or do you want me to pick some other ones? I tried to put the ones together that I thought matched. Mommy lets me match her clothes, so I'm pretty good at matching."

"Abi, just how many did you get out?" Georgiana asked, but Dana could tell she wasn't perturbed with her daughter's enthusiasm. On the contrary, her smile said she found Abi's assistance adorable. And so did Dana.

"Just a few. I didn't know what Miss Dana's favorite color is, so I tried to get something in every color."

Georgiana laughed. "I see."

"How about that blue shirt with the flowers on it, and those jeans there?" Dana pointed to the outfit.

"Okay." Abi gathered the two items and handed them over. "I'll put the other stuff back, Mommy."

"Thanks, sweetie. And you can come down to the kitchen when you get done, and we'll finish getting dinner ready."

"Okay."

Georgiana moved back into the hall with Dana by her side. "If you'd like to come down after you're dressed, and if you'd feel like helping with dinner, I can always use a hand in the kitchen."

Dana rarely saw the kitchen at her apartment. She either ate out or grabbed a toasted bagel and coffee on the go. John had probably told Landon and Georgiana about her background if they weren't aware already, so this woman knew that Dana was a fish out of water on the farm. But Georgiana graciously and kindly allowed her to ease into their world. Dana's gratitude was instant. "I'd like that very much."

Georgiana turned to go down the stairs, but Dana remembered something she'd said earlier that she hadn't understood. "Georgiana?"

"Yes?"

"You said we'd eat dinner before John goes to work."

She nodded. "He works the third shift at the steel plant, three nights on, four nights off. Tonight is night two of his three on. He's also taking business classes during the week, getting his degree at the college in

Stockville. Of course you knew that, since you met him in one of the college's online business forums, right?"

"Right."

"But yes, he works, goes to school, helps us run the fish camp and also does his share around the farm." Georgiana's mouth flattened, and she took a step back toward Dana. "As I said earlier, Landon was really touched by everything John did while Landon was overseas, and everything John still does to help things run smoothly around here." She bit her lower lip. "Can I be honest with you?"

Dana heard the worry in her tone. "Yes, please."

"Landon wasn't certain how to feel about your coming down here, leaving Chicago and your business and all to head to Alabama and help John start a dude ranch. See, John was so disheartened when the bank turned down his business plan, and then he met you, and he got his hopes up again."

"I believe his business will be successful," Dana assured her. "That's why I'm here, to make certain he has everything he needs to get it running. And it's an investment for Brooks International—our first investment of this type." The first of many, if Dana planned to follow through with her father's last wish. As long as she could show her brother that the business could turn a profit, she should be able to assist many aspiring entrepreneurs all over the country.

"I know. And now that you're here, and I've heard how happy John sounds and can practically feel his excitement over the dude ranch, well, Landon and I believe that you may be the answer to our prayer for John."

Dana wasn't sure what to say. "Your prayer?"

"Yes," Georgiana said. "Our prayer that this time, *his* dreams can come true."

Chapter Three

John ate every bite of his dinner but hardly tasted the steak and potatoes. His attention had been held captive by Dana Brooks's excitement over his business plan. He'd sensed her interest on the college forum and even heard it in her voice when they'd talked on the phone, but he hadn't been able to *see* her passion for the project. However, with every mention of the dude ranch tonight, her eyes lit up, her smile stretched wide and her enthusiasm became palpable. Over *his* idea.

Now that they'd finished eating and Landon and Georgiana had gone upstairs to get Abi ready for bed, he knew he should head to the cabin and get a couple hours' sleep before he had to go to work at the steel plant. But he didn't want to leave.

More than that, he didn't want to leave Dana.

"You want to go out on the porch for a while? It's a clear night, should be able to see the stars." His voice sounded awkward, like a kid nervously asking a girl out on a date, but she didn't seem to notice.

"Sure. It isn't often we get a good view of the stars in the city. All the lights drown them out, make them harder to see."

"Well, as long as it isn't cloudy, you can almost always see them here." He opened the door and looked up to see that there wasn't a cloud in the sky, and the sky was, sure enough, covered with stars.

She followed him out and they sat in two of the wooden rockers that lined the porch, where the sound of Abi's laughter echoed from the upstairs window.

"Sounds like she's enjoying her bedtime story," Dana said.

"Landon tickles her as he tucks her in." John grinned as his niece's giggles subsided, and he heard the soft whispers of Abi saying her prayers with her parents.

Dana moved a hand to her heart. "Oh, that's so precious."

"Yeah, it is."

The prayers eventually ended, and the two of them rocked in silence, chairs creaking as they moved back and forth. John enjoyed sharing the peaceful setting with the city girl. He didn't know if she viewed the place the way he did, if she noticed the things he did, but right now he took comfort in the sky blanketed with stars, the barn and fields highlighted by the full moon, the sounds of bulls bellowing, horses nickering, a breeze whispering through the trees and the oddly harmonic melody of crickets and frogs.

Did she see this as beautiful, as he did? He started to ask her, but halted when she emitted a single, breathy, "Wow."

John stretched his legs out in front of him, leaned back in the rocker and grinned. "I was thinking the same thing."

"It's amazing here, isn't it? So peaceful, so beautiful."

He crossed his feet at the ankles, noticed a few white Charolais cattle in the distance glowing beneath the moonlight. "Yes, it is."

"Growing up, Ryan and I traveled quite a bit with our father, until he became too sick to leave home. We'd go from one business venture to another, have an occasional vacation, usually tropical locations because Daddy really liked the beach. But everything was always—" she shook her head "—I don't know how to describe it…"

John knew how he described it. "Busy?"

Her white-blond hair, luminescent in the moonlight, shifted against her shoulders as she nodded. "Yes, busy. Noisy. And even though we were supposed to be relaxing, I don't remember it that way. But this is so serene."

John found it extremely satisfying to hear her describe his own feelings about the ranch. MaciJo had considered the setting boring, a place where no one would want to stay for life. In fact, the one girl he'd fallen for had been determined to find a way out of Claremont, and she'd done just that when she got the scholarship to Vanderbilt. But Dana knew everything about life in the city and about life with an abundance of money—something else MaciJo had wanted that John couldn't provide—yet she appreciated the tranquillity and simplicity of the ranch. "One thing I remember most about my parents," he said. "They called this place God's country. I'd have to agree."

"Georgiana mentioned that your parents had passed on and that you handled the farm and took over raising your younger brother while Landon was overseas." She pushed back in the rocker, then added, "That must have been hard."

She had no idea. John should've realized that Georgiana had probably filled her in on his past. Women had a natural urge to share, and John had hardly revealed anything about that time with anyone. But hearing her bring it up brought back the memories of those years and how he'd struggled to make ends meet. He'd been so focused on work and holding on to the farm that he'd almost lost Casey, both physically and spiritually.

"I'm sorry. I shouldn't have asked," she said, and John realized that he'd been so caught up in the painful memories that he hadn't answered her.

"No, it's okay. It's just that I went through a lot then, but we made it. With God's help, Casey and I made it."

"What happened?"

John swallowed, unsure of how much he wanted to tell. Sure, he'd been chatting online and talking on the phone with her for several months, but he didn't really know her yet, and he hadn't opened up with anyone about how difficult that time had been.

She cleared her throat. "You probably don't want to talk about it. I guess it's because I didn't have much of a family—just my father and my brother—that I feel drawn to know about other family relationships. But I shouldn't have asked."

Typically he would say that it was okay, and stop at that, but for some reason he felt closer to Dana than he had with anyone in a very long time, and he felt compelled to share the rest. "I couldn't pay the bills with money from the farm, so I took another job at the feed store and then another job working the third shift at the steel plant, the job I still have."

"You were working around the clock, weren't you?" Her rocker creaked as she leaned toward him. "Like the schedule you still have now?"

"My schedule now is a breeze compared to life back then. It was tough, and I didn't handle it that well." He tilted his head to see if he heard any voices from inside the house, and he heard the faint sound of Georgiana and Landon talking. He was glad they were occupied, because he wouldn't want Landon to hear this confession. Sure, Landon knew John had had a hard time, but he'd never told his older brother how guilty he felt about Casey's accident.

She shifted again in her seat, her body language telling him that she was interested in his past and in his struggles. "Sounds like you didn't sleep much back then, either," she said.

"I got enough, but sleeping wasn't the issue. Not being there for Casey—that was the bigger problem." He let the emotions he'd pushed to the recesses of his mind and heart ease forward and continued. "He got in with a bad crowd, turned away from his faith, away from me, and turned to alcohol." John took a deep breath, pushed it out. "I was so focused on work that I didn't even realize I was losing him, not until he got behind the wheel drunk. He had his girlfriend with him, our preacher's granddaughter, Nadia."

She stopped rocking, and although he turned his focus to the fields, he could sense that the woman next to him had turned her full attention to him. "Did he— did they have an accident?"

John nodded. "He was speeding when they hit a tree not far from where you had your accident today. Casey was banged up, but he was okay. But for a while there, we didn't know if Nadia would make it. I've never begged God so hard to help, to heal her and forgive Casey. And to forgive me." He hadn't admitted the blame to anyone, but he did now. Oddly, relief flooded him with the admission.

"I'm so glad they were both okay." She paused. "Casey is better now?"

Pride at how far Casey had come since that horrible night filled John's soul. "Found God again and turned away from the wild group at school. Got the grades he needed to get accepted to Alabama, and he's doing well there. He's taken an interest in web design and has already created a few websites. His first semester was in the fall, and he made the dean's list." He grinned.

She smiled. "And Nadia?"

"She's at the high school. She's a year younger, but they are still dating. He comes home every few weeks to see her. It's only a couple of hours' drive from Tuscaloosa."

"That's wonderful. And I'm guessing your relationship with Casey is stronger, too, because of what you went through together? Going through hard times brings people closer, doesn't it?"

"Yes, it does." John still didn't look at her, but kept his attention on the fields, the moonlight, the grazing livestock. Surprised at himself for opening up this much, he didn't think he could look at her now, because if he did, she might see too much, become too close. He'd kept his distance from others, particularly from women, since the pain of MaciJo. Working around the clock and tending to the farm helped him maintain his distance and kept his dating to a minimum, but over the next few weeks he suspected he'd spend more time with Dana Brooks than he had with any female in the past decade. And the fact that he felt comfortable with her, comfortable enough to tell her about the guilt of Casey's accident, didn't bode well. Because in a month, she'd go back to the city. He cleared his throat, prepared to tell her that he should head home and get some sleep before his shift started at the steel plant.

But then her words stopped his progress.

"I never went through any hard times like that, didn't have any struggles in life at all, until those last weeks with my father. And it's sad to say that I don't think we ever really knew each other until we went through that time together. Maybe it was because my mother died when I was born that he didn't want to open up, didn't want to get hurt again. But even though I was with him often, I didn't really know him until he realized he was dying." She remembered those last weeks, when he finally acknowledged what was important and tried so hard to make sure she understood and didn't make the same mistakes that he'd made. "I just wish we'd had more time together like that, and I wish Ryan would have spent more time with him then, instead of concentrating so much on keeping the company going while Daddy was sick."

She barely held back her tears, and when John finally turned and looked at her, his golden eyes filled with understanding, her tears slipped free. He'd opened up to her tonight, and now she'd done the same, telling him more than she'd shared with anyone but Ryan. And her brother hadn't understood, no matter how many times she'd tried to explain the change their father had undergone before he died, but the handsome cowboy sitting next to her on the porch did.

He leaned toward her, reached out and rested his hand on top of hers. The warmth of his palm covered her skin, his fingers gently wrapping around the sides of her hand. "It's good you got to spend that time with him."

"I feel as if I just dumped a lot on you," she said, blinking past the tears and forcing a smile. "Don't know what came over me."

He returned the smile, the mood shifting and the tension between them easing with the gesture. Then he squeezed the top of her hand before sliding his away. "It's the open country, sitting on the porch and having no reason to hold back on your thoughts and feelings. Kind of like sitting out by an open campfire and sharing all your secrets."

"The kind of thing you'd do at a dude ranch, right?"

"Exactly." He straightened in the rocker, scooted forward and Dana knew he was about to leave. "You still think my dude ranch will work?"

"I wouldn't be here if I didn't. And it'll be very rewarding when I prove to my brother that I picked a wise investment."

His smile grew, dimples popping into place, and he stood. "So Ryan Brooks doubted the success of an Alabama dude ranch? After six banks all thought it was a terrific idea and couldn't wait to loan me money? In fact, I've still got all their letters of praise telling me why it's a fabulous idea, if he'd like to see them." At her soft laughter, John added, "Seriously, I do appreciate your taking a chance on this, especially when no one else would."

"I'm making an investment based on my instinct more than on marketing history, of course, but Daddy told me to follow what feels right." She pushed a lock of hair behind her ear. "And this feels right."

"Investing in an Alabama dude ranch?"

She wanted to make sure he understood and put a lot of thought into her words. "The dude ranch is what's on the surface, but that's not what I'm investing in."

He'd taken a step toward leaving, but he stopped and turned, leaned against the porch post. "You aren't investing in the dude ranch?"

The moonlight behind him created a beautifully sculpted cowboy silhouette, but even in the shadow, she could see the question in his eyes, the slight tilt in his face saying he wondered if she'd changed her mind. That couldn't be further from the truth. On the contrary, after learning even more about this intriguing man tonight and seeing how deeply he cared for others and how strongly he felt about this beautiful ranch, she'd reaffirmed her decision.

"My father always said that when you invest, you aren't investing in things, you're investing in the heart behind the product, in the soul that makes it work. I'm not investing in an Alabama dude ranch. I'm investing in you."

He took another step then turned, and even though his face was in shadow, Dana knew he smiled at her now. "I plan to show you that's a wise investment," he said.

She returned his smile. "I'm counting on it."

Chapter Four

"Yay! I knew Uncle John would come watch me ride!" Abi waved wildly, toppled a little in the saddle and had to regain her balance on the brown mare. "Whoa!"

Dana's cell phone buzzed in her pocket, but she ignored the interruption and watched Abi find her seat in the saddle again. Ryan had been texting ever since she woke up this morning, and she'd had enough business distractions. Today was Saturday, a day normal people relaxed and enjoyed life. Normal people, like the Cutter family. And she wanted to enjoy it, too, especially now that she saw John's old blue pickup coming up the drive.

"Abi, you need to pay attention." Georgiana stood next to Dana against the round pen railing. "I'm guessing she nearly fell off the horse trying to wave to John."

"You'd guess right, but she's back on track now." Dana continued to be amazed with everything Georgiana could do and sense without sight. She'd even hiked the trail between the Cutter farm and Georgiana's mother's farm without assistance or complaint.

But even though Dana answered Georgiana, her eyes hadn't left the blue pickup nearing the barn. John didn't wear his Stetson today, his brown waves ruffling in the breeze from the open truck window. "I thought you said he would sleep this morning since he worked all night." Dana pulled her cell from her pocket, deleted Ryan's text instructing her to call him and glanced at the time. "It's only ten o'clock. Didn't he work until seven?"

"Yes, he did." Georgiana shook her head as though she didn't know what to do with her brother-in-law. "And he probably didn't rest before making sure all the guests at the camp were set for fishing before he came over. Landon checked them all in before he left, but John would've wanted to meet everyone, too, and verify that they all found a good fishing spot."

"They're both very hands-on with the business, aren't they?" Dana thought it'd be nice if Ryan would take a lesson from John and Landon. They checked on their business this morning, but then they went about enjoying the day. She could almost see her brother, rising at the crack of dawn and moving to the office in his apartment with a cup of coffee and a bagel, then proceeding to work the entire day. Tomorrow he'd do it all again.

"Since we're the only ones running the camp, and since that business is what we're banking on to save the farm, they have to be hands-on," Georgiana said with a laugh. "But they both enjoy working, especially when they can see the fruits of their labor. They'll work hard on the dude ranch, too."

"I know they will." Dana had sensed that ambition,

that drive, in the very first conversation she'd had with John. And the little bit she'd seen and learned since arriving in Alabama only solidified that initial impression.

John climbed out of the truck and walked toward the round pen. He wore a green Western shirt and blue jeans, strong legs flexing against the worn denim with every step. Dana caught herself doing a flirty finger wave that probably made her look like she was still in high school. Shocked at her girly reaction to the gorgeous cowboy, she dropped her hand to the rail and gripped the wood.

What was it about John Cutter? She'd hardly slept last night after their intense conversation, and she wondered if he felt the same way she did about sharing so much so soon, as if a bandage had been ripped off and he could see her every wound. Then again, she'd heard that sometimes a wound needed air to heal. She did feel better about life in general this morning…and about spending the next month with the good-looking cowboy who intrigued her not only with his looks, but also with his heart.

"And I said that John *should* sleep, not that he would. I also told my daughter not to call and ask him to come, because he refuses to tell the child no." She raised her voice. "Abi, did you call Uncle John?"

"No, ma'am. You told me not to." She trotted a little farther away. "I texted him."

"You *texted* him?"

"Abi has a phone?" Dana knew lots of kids had

phones nowadays, but it didn't seem like a necessity for a seven-year-old country girl.

"No, she doesn't, though she asks for one at every opportunity." Georgiana took a step up on the railing. "Mom, did you let Abi use your cell?"

Eden Sanders, Georgiana's mother, gave riding lessons to Abi and a few other kids her age. At Georgiana's question, she looked undeniably guilty. "Abi asked to borrow it when y'all got here. I thought she was playing a game or something. Should've known she'd try to get John to come since Landon couldn't make it. She likes showing off for the guys." Eden laughed. "Guess she's a lot like her mama that way."

"Hey, I never showed off."

"Sure you did, but we all thought it was cute." John's boots thudded solidly against the ground as he made his way from the barn. "Especially my older brother."

"Uncle John, did you see that? Grandma is letting me gallop on Brownie now! Look at me go!"

He applauded the adorable redhead as he walked. "I did see, and you're doing a great job."

"She knew her daddy had to run to the feed store this morning and couldn't come, and she also knew her uncle John needed to sleep." Georgiana raised her voice. "Isn't that right, Abi?"

Abi acted as if she didn't hear her mother, but her little smirk said she did.

"Ah, sleep is overrated." John stepped up to the railing next to Dana, his warmth sending a tremor of awareness along her side, as did his height. Most guys either matched her five-nine or stood slightly taller, so that she usually saw eye to eye with them when she was wearing heels. But John Cutter stood an easy six-two, six-four with his boots. "How about you? Did you sleep okay at the farm?" His words, low and rich, were delivered close to her left ear. Close enough that his warm breath teased her neck.

She felt her cheeks flush. "Yes, I slept fine." That was a lie, but it slipped out before she could think of an appropriate way to explain that she'd barely slept at all for thinking of him—not only the way his heartfelt story had touched her last night but also the way he made her feel, period. She'd gone to her room after he left the porch, but she'd only moved to the open window to get another view of John, riding Red across the field in the moonlight. When she finally drifted off to sleep, she'd seen herself on the back of the saddle, her arms around his waist and her worries about marketing strategies, business planning and future acquisitions left behind as they rode off into the distance.

"Dana, you okay? Did you hear me?"

She realized he must have asked her something else, but she was so caught up in her daydreams—of him— that she hadn't heard the question. "I'm sorry, what?"

He grinned as though he knew what she'd been thinking. Thank goodness he didn't.

"I asked if you took out any more livestock on your way over to Ms. Sanders's farm."

"No, of course not." She playfully punched his arm, and then swallowed thickly when her knuckles collided with firm biceps.

"We hiked, silly," Georgiana said. "And stop teasing

her. Gypsy was ready to go, anyway. Dana put her out of her misery by helping it happen quickly."

He tapped Dana's shoulder. "See, I told you."

Abi passed by them again. She wore a pink riding helmet, a blue T-shirt, jeans and pink cowboy boots. The bubblegum shade of her helmet made her red curls appear even more vivid. "I'm doing good, huh?"

John, noticing the question was directed solely to him, answered, "Yes, you are."

Georgiana stepped down from the rail. "She wants to practice every day now. Ever since *someone* told her that she would be demonstrating riding for kids visiting the dude ranch, she thinks she has to practice nonstop. I can hardly get her to do anything else, and that includes cleaning her room and doing her homework."

John managed to turn his laugh into something that sounded like he'd cleared his throat. "I wonder who told her that."

"Yeah, I wonder." Georgiana attempted to sound mad, but failed and ended up smiling. "I do love hearing how excited she is about helping out with the dude ranch. I mean, she likes visiting the pond when the fish camp guests are there, but I know she'll like the dude ranch even better, since she'll have such an active role. That was sweet of you to include her like that."

"I'm looking forward to having her help." John gave Abi a thumbs-up as she circled the outer edge of the pen. "One of the families who checked in at the fish camp this morning has two little girls about Abi's age. I told them I was sure my niece would come see them when she got back from her riding lessons."

"No doubt. Hey, maybe that will give her a reason to leave. I have a ton of work to do at the house." Georgiana leaned over the rail again. "Abi, are you ready to go? Uncle John said there are some girls your age at the fish camp. You could go visit them."

"Not yet." She trotted past them once more. "I'm still practicing."

Georgiana sighed. "Okay, I'm going in Grandma's house until you finish." She turned toward John and Dana. "Y'all want to come inside or are you staying out here?"

"Actually, I thought I might take Dana to go see the land for the dude ranch, show her the plans for the campsites, trail rides and all today. Or at least get started." He looked at Dana. "That okay with you?"

"Yes, that's fine." She knew she should tell him that they could see everything another day so he could sleep today, since he'd had no more than three hours—tops. But the prospect of spending time with him caused her to keep that idea to herself.

"Okay. Abi and I will see you later at the farm. And, John," Georgiana said, "I know you're a grown man, but I still feel the need to remind you that you need to sleep sometime."

"Uh-huh."

She lifted a shoulder. "Someone needs to watch after you. Landon and I try…"

Winking at Dana, John cut her off midsentence. "And I appreciate it."

Dana swallowed, thought how she wouldn't mind being the one to watch after the dashing cowboy. Then she shook the thought away. Her home was in Chicago. Her work and her only remaining family member were there, too, and she'd be going back in a month. She'd be wise to keep those facts at the front of her mind at all times.

John leaned over the rail, his side brushing against Dana's in the process, and all thoughts of Chicago vanished. Why should she worry about going back in a month, anyway? She should enjoy being in Alabama, right here, right now, with John.

"Abi, Miss Dana and I are going back to the farm so I can show her some of the dude ranch stuff. We'll see you in a little bit, okay?"

His adorable niece trotted closer. "Okay, but don't forget when y'all test the camping out, I get to come, too, right? You promised. And I have spring break the week after next, so we have to go either before I leave or after I get back from seeing Daddy in Florida."

"Don't worry. We'll make sure you're here for camping. Now you keep practicing and don't let Brownie buck you off."

Abi laughed, sending copper freckles spilling across her cheeks with her smile. "She doesn't even know how to buck, do you, Brownie?" She stroked the horse's mane, and Brownie nickered happily. "See? She said no."

"Abi, it's your turn, honey." Her grandmother motioned for her to join the other kids on horses at the opposite end of the round pen.

"Gotta go." She turned Brownie and headed back toward the others.

"Did you already go shopping, or are those some of the clothes you brought from Chicago?" He indicated her outfit as they walked toward the truck.

Dana glanced down at the red gingham shirt, jeans and boots. "I brought the jeans from home, but Georgiana let me borrow the shirt and the boots. I was lucky that we wear the same size shoes."

He gave her an appraising glance. "Yeah, those boots look right at home on you. In fact, if I didn't know better, I'd say you were a true-blue country girl."

Dana had received a lot of compliments from men over the years, but "true blue country girl" had never made it to the list before. Oddly, it flattered her more than any she could remember. "Thanks."

"You're welcome." He walked to the passenger side and opened her door. Dana caught a hint of an undeniably masculine scent that caused her to inhale deeper. She was used to the strong, spicy scents some of the men she'd dated wore. But those came across as manufactured and fake. John's scent was real. In fact, she wondered if he wore any cologne at all, or if *that* was simply the way Alabama cowboys smelled.

He rounded the front of the truck and climbed in. Then he glanced at her and lifted a brow.

"What?" she asked.

"You going to tell me what you're thinking, or am I supposed to ignore those looks?"

Her hand moved to her mouth, as though she could push the look back in. What had she done, anyway, when she daydreamed about them riding horses in the moonlight earlier or just now, when she'd practically lost herself in his amazing scent? Had she smiled? What if she'd made that flirty sound of appreciation that her sorority sisters had often made at Georgetown when they saw a frat boy who got their attention? Dana had promised herself she'd never make a sound like that. She'd always been the cool one, the one to remain aloof regardless of impressive muscles or alluring smiles.

She moved her hand to her throat and prayed it hadn't betrayed her with any flirtatious noises directed at John.

He laughed. "Don't panic. You just looked a little surprised, that's all." He fished the keys from his jeans pocket. "All city girls as jittery as you?"

Jittery? Dana Ellen Brooks? Never. Or never…until she'd arrived at the Cutter farm. "I wasn't panicked. And I was surprised because—" she racked her brain for a way to complete the sentence "—because I'm not used to guys opening the door for me."

And that was the honest truth. The guys she dated typically didn't open the car door, because they relied on the valet to do it. Plus, she'd never been all that close to any one guy, because none of them were interested in her; they were all interested in Brooks International. But John opened her door out of pure respect, and it had nothing to do with her last name. In fact, she'd wager he opened the door for all females.

"Obviously those guys up north need a lesson in manners." He tossed up a hand and waved goodbye to Abi, then cranked the engine.

"Obviously." She smiled, relieved to get out of that awkward conversation. Ryan and her father had always praised her ability to maintain her composure in the most heated business meetings. You would think she could keep it together around John.

He reached across the seat, pulled at the strap beside her right arm. "We might only be going to the next farm, but you should still buckle up."

She nodded, unable to speak with his face so close to hers.

Yes, you would think she could keep it together. Probably a good thing she didn't plan on moving down here for good. Too much Southern rancher couldn't be good for her heart. Her pulse raced almost as much as when she ran the Chicago marathon.

He moved back to his side then pushed the gearshift that sprouted from the floor. His hands were as masculine as the rest of him, nothing at all like the hands of the businessmen she typically dealt with up north. No doubt the inside of his palms bore calluses from hard work. Dana thought of what it'd be like to hold his hand, to feel the evidence of his daily labor against the softness of her palm.

"We may not be able to ride all the trails today, but we can at least take in a couple."

She eased her eyes from his hand to his face. "We've got plenty of time." But inside she knew that wasn't true, and she wished she'd persuaded Ryan to agree to her spending more than a month in Alabama. She didn't know why she felt so loopy around John Cutter, but she wanted enough time to figure it out.

He left the Sanders's driveway and drove toward the Cutter farm, where the fishing camp guests were enjoying the beautiful weather by the pond.

"Hey, Mr. John!" A little girl in overalls and brown pigtails waved as John drove down the dirt drive. She handed her fishing pole to her mother and ran toward the fence with a younger version of herself following close behind.

John slowed the truck. "Hey, you're Carrie, right?"

"Yes, sir, and this is Ashley." She pointed to the little girl sprinting up behind her.

"Are y'all catching anything?"

Dana noticed his voice softened when he spoke to the little girl, the same way it softened when he spoke to Abi.

The younger girl piped up. "I caught the biggest one, Mr. John!" Her shoulders dropped a notch. "But Carrie's was prettier."

The older girl nodded solidly. "Yep, Ashley caught the biggest but mine is the prettiest."

"Its shales sparkle like glitter." Each *s* was slurred, making little Ashley even more adorable.

Carrie shook her head. "Not shales, Ashley. *Scales.*"

"Right, scales." Ashley grinned, displaying two missing front teeth, no doubt the reason for her precious slur.

"And I baited my hook one time, too," Carrie said with pride. "The way you showed us this morning. Ashley won't bait hers."

"It's yucky!"

John laughed at the pair. "This is Miss Dana. She's staying at the farm for a few weeks."

"Wow, weeks?" Carrie's dark eyes grew wide. "I wish we could stay for weeks."

"We've got school," Ashley explained, "but I like school, too."

"That's because you're in kindergarten. Just wait until you're in third grade and do real work. Then you won't like it at all."

"Yes, I will." Ashley stuck her chin out as though daring her big sister to contradict her.

Carrie ignored the gesture. "But we've got spring break next week, and Daddy said we're having so much fun we might come back then."

"That'd be great." John turned his attention to their parents. "Y'all have everything you need?"

"Everything's wonderful," the mom answered, and the dad nodded.

"Well, if you want to come back for spring break, just let me know. We still have two cabins available."

"Put me down for one of them," the man responded.

Dana noticed three other families waving from spots farther around the pond. One had a huge picnic basket, the entire family diving into sandwiches, chips and drinks.

John waved back. "Let me know if y'all need anything, or you can help yourself, as I told you this morning. Pretty much anything you'll need is either on my porch or in the shed. Minnow tank is around back if you want more for your buckets."

"Thanks!" several of them yelled, and John proceeded down the driveway.

Dana thought of the references to spring break, particularly Abi's reference. "Abi said she was going to Florida for spring break?"

"Georgiana's ex-husband, Abi's father, lives in Tampa. Abi's spending spring break there."

"Oh." Dana didn't want to pry, but John must have known she was curious.

"Georgiana married the wrong guy the first time around. She should've married Landon, but she didn't." He tilted his head as though deciding how to explain. "Anyway, she married a guy who wanted a perfect wife, and when Georgiana went blind, he didn't see her that way anymore and found someone else he deemed perfect."

"That's terrible."

"Yeah, but she's got it right now." His easy smile said he was happy for his brother and Georgiana…and Abi.

"But they seemed to have worked everything out okay with visitation and all for Abi," Dana said.

"Yeah, he comes up once a month and picks her up for a weekend, takes her back to Tampa. He usually flies, but I think he's driving this time since they have an entire week. Abi said he wants to show her a few things on the way back down." He shrugged. "Sight-seeing and all."

"That sounds nice."

He waited a telling beat. "I guess. The thing is, Pete's different from Claremont folks. He's from here, but he tries to act like he isn't."

Dana twisted in the seat to see him better. "What do you mean?"

"You know, dresses all in name brands, drives a fancy car, brags about all the places he's been. He'll take Abi to a bunch of impressive places while he has her—" his mouth flattened "—tries to show he can give her more than Landon can."

For a moment there, Dana could've said he was describing nearly every guy and girl she'd known in Chicago. But then his last statement told her that more than the guy's ego irritated John. The fact that he attempted to make Landon look bad infuriated him.

Her admiration swelled. "Well, if you ask me, Abi looks like she couldn't be happier than when she's on the ranch. I don't know if I've ever met such a joyful little girl."

His face relaxed, the hint of a dimple shadowing his right cheek as he bit back a smile of pride. "We may not be as successful in business as Pete, but we do try to make her happy."

"I'm not so sure you can say that about your and Landon's business skills. The fishing camp is a hit."

He released the smile, and both deep dimples popped into place. "Yeah, it is, isn't it?"

"No doubt." Dana peered out the back window until she could no longer see the array of families around the pond. She'd taken a lot of trips growing up, most of them to five-star resorts and beach condominiums owned by her family, but she'd never done anything remotely similar to the fishing day that each of those families currently experienced by the pond. They'd all been smiling, enjoying one another's company on the beautiful day. She, Ryan and their father had had a good time together, in much the same way that Abi would enjoy time with her father during spring break, but they'd never done anything that she'd consider "normal" family fun. Everything was bigger, over-the-top, extravagant. *"We're making a major memory here,"* her father always said.

But she wondered if a few smaller memories would've made more of an impact. All the palm-tree laden resorts ran together, to where she barely knew what continent they'd been on, much less what country. And her father always worked in a business meeting or two during the trip, though he had plenty of staff and nannies for Dana and Ryan.

Dana thought about the little girl so excited about baiting her own hook and realized that she'd never even held a fishing pole. Or had a reason to ask her daddy to help her bait her own hook.

Her throat tightened, and she turned to peer out the passenger window at the fields passing by. Blinked several times at the scene of white cattle and brown horses…and concentrated on not letting herself cry.

"Does that sound okay, to take a couple of the horses through the trails and see what you think, then check out the area I plan to have graded for the campsites down by the creek?"

She blinked. "Yes, that sounds great."

"You ride, right? I saw photos of you riding online. I noticed you ride English, but Western shouldn't be that much of a stretch."

"I do ride English." That'd been the thing to do at her boarding school. She'd enjoyed the school and enjoyed riding, but now the entire thing sounded pretentious, even to her own ears. "But I've always wanted to ride Western. And I'd love to see the trails that your guests will ride." Her cell buzzed in her pocket. It'd been going off sporadically throughout their time at the Sanders's farm and then during the drive to John's farm, but she'd ignored Ryan's texts. She withdrew the phone, took another look at the display to make sure it wasn't an emergency.

Call me. We got the Miami deal. That was your baby. Wanted to tell you instead of text you, but you aren't responding. What are you doing down there, anyway? I need your input. This is huge. Press release going out tonight. BTW, Dad would want you here, not in the sticks. I don't care what you think. Get done down there and get home.

Dana deleted the message, then promptly received another.

Probably sounded harsh. I do love you, sis. But I want you back here. I need your help. And Dad would want you here, too.

"Everything okay?" John asked, stopping the truck beside the big red barn.

She deleted the new message. "No—" she swallowed "—everything isn't okay."

"Anything I can do to help?"

She nodded, looked into those honey-colored eyes and knew that spending time with him today, riding the trails and enjoying the beauty of this incredible ranch, would definitely help. A couple of horses had moved

to their paddocks when the truck approached. She suspected they wanted to ride, to feel free, as much as
Dana. "Yes, I believe you can help. Take me on a trail
ride?"

Dimples flashed with his smile. "That's the plan."

Chapter Five

John had thought they would stick to the easiest, lower-elevation paths today while Dana got accustomed to riding the trails, but she was a natural and they quickly progressed higher on Lookout Mountain. "You doing okay?" He'd asked the question sporadically throughout their journey, and each time received essentially the same response.

"I'm wonderful. This is so incredible. Your guests are going to love it!"

Her enthusiasm was contagious, and he found himself believing even more in the potential for an Alabama dude ranch. In a few weeks, his business plan would become a bona fide, honest-to-goodness, moneymaking venture. Plus, he'd be doing something he loved in the process. And he owed it all to this fascinating woman.

Dana rode Fallon, Georgiana's palomino, and she looked like a princess sitting astride the stunning mare, with Fallon's gold pelt and white mane glistening in the occasional spears of sunlight through the trees. Dana's white-blond hair dazzled in those bursts of light, as though God shone His personal spotlight through the forest to force John to look at the striking woman.

He didn't need a spotlight. John had a hard time taking his eyes off Dana Brooks, not only because of her beauty, but also because of her intelligence and, even more than that, her acceptance of his world. Her blue eyes scanned the mountain in unconcealed awe, with occasional gasps of appreciation for the breathtaking scenes. He could hardly wait to hear what she thought of the view around the next curve in the trail. It didn't surprise him that she noticed the scent even before she saw the source.

"Oh, my. What is that?" She inhaled deeply, a soft smile playing around the corners of her mouth and her eyes closing momentarily as she absorbed the sweet fragrance. "It's—" another deep inhalation "—wonderful."

He grinned, once again taken aback by her enjoyment of the simple things, the God-made things, that had always touched his heart and soul. "They're supposed to be the most fragrant of any blooms. Of course, when you have this many in one place, they're easier to smell." He guided Red around the curve then watched to see Dana's reaction when she saw the burst of color hiding in the forest. "Rhododendrons. *This* is what makes this trail my favorite."

"Oh, my." Her mouth dropped open and she shook her head in amazement at the towering trees bordering both sides of the path. Vivid purple, hot-pink and bright red blooms completely saturated the branches, giving the impression they'd ridden into the middle of a rainbow. "I've never seen anything like this."

"This is the only place I know of where they are this intense. Usually you'll find a patch of a single color—purple, red or pink, sometimes white—but I haven't seen the colors melded together anywhere but here, on this trail. I'm thinking it'll appeal to our guests."

"Absolutely. It's more extravagant than any botanical gardens I've ever visited, because they're so huge and so real. Right here, growing in their natural state and truly flourishing. It's like a kaleidoscope, isn't it? Especially in the areas where the sun's rays touch the blooms through the trees. Are you going to name the trails? This could be the Rhododendron Trail, or something to do with all this color. Maybe the Kaleidoscope Trail. I think that'd be a great idea, and you could provide a map for guests to see all the trails on the mountain, like the ski lodges have for skiing."

"I've never been skiing, but I have seen the resort maps online and had thought we'd do something similar here. They color-code them, don't they, based on difficulty?"

She blinked. "You haven't skied? They have skiing in Tennessee, you know, and North Carolina. That isn't very far away."

John didn't want to make her feel bad, but the distance wasn't the problem. And her comment was a subtle reminder of the differences in their worlds. "No, it isn't that far, but it's tough to leave the farm. The animals need tending, and—" he might as well say it "—skiing is pricey."

Her pretty brows dipped, mouth flattened. "Oh. Right. I hadn't thought about that."

He was certain she'd never had to think about anything that had to do with a lack of money, but he also knew she hadn't meant to offend him with the remark. And John didn't take offense. Sure, he'd love to see a little more of the world, would love to do things like ski and visit a beach, but those types of trips didn't fit into a struggling rancher's budget. And he found his happiness right here, amid the fields, the livestock, the mountains, the creeks and the abundance of God's beauty, like the rhododendrons surrounding them now. "I've never hurt for anything, and I can't imagine anything much prettier than what we've got on the ranch."

She smiled, apparently glad that he hadn't been hurt by her remark. "I don't think *I've* ever seen anything prettier than what you have on the ranch, either."

John believed her. The pleasure he saw on her face right now wasn't fake; she truly saw the ranch as beautiful.

Dana guided Fallon closer to the blooms. The mare pushed her head amid the trees, sniffed a large purple blossom then sneezed with gusto. "Oh, I'm sorry, girl." Dana ran a hand down Fallon's neck.

"Don't let her fool you. Fallon likes the way they smell." And sure enough, the palomino stuck her nose in another bloom before sneezing again. "Even if they make her sneeze."

Dana continued stroking Fallon's neck then leaned forward to inhale a bright pink bloom. "I can't blame her for wanting the full effect. They smell wonderful."

"Some folks say they smell like root beer, but I never got that." John inhaled, thinking the scent too floral for the tart drink.

"Root beer? Really? They're much more feminine than that, floral but almost sweet, like sugar candy." She tenderly cradled a bloom in her palm. "Heady, isn't it? This scent? Can you imagine a wedding with these flowers all around? No one would pay attention to the bride and groom. Roses are pretty, but these are exceptional."

"Never seen rhododendrons at a wedding." He'd thought that Dana was different from every female he'd ever known, and she was in a way, growing up as part of an affluent family in a big city. But her comment reminded him that she was still every bit as feminine as the girls in Claremont, a girl who saw flowers and thought of weddings. Probably dreamed about getting married, too, to some guy she'd met up in Chicago. A fellow who wore a suit each day, drove a fancy car and took her to upscale restaurants. But even so, she sure looked right at home sitting in Fallon's saddle and admiring the natural beauty of Lookout Mountain.

"We need to make sure we have photos of these trees for the ranch website." She touched another pink bloom. "You might even have people who'd want to get married here, in the middle of this path. Then we could name this the Wedding Trail." She sniffed the bloom again. "Wouldn't that be romantic? Several of my sorority sisters from college had outdoor weddings, and they were nice, but nothing like this. This would be amazing."

"Getting married on a dude ranch?" John couldn't

see it, at all, and he couldn't disguise the skepticism in his tone. "Don't get me wrong, I think we should market every angle we can, but I'm not sure folks would be willing to hike up the mountain or ride horses to get married here, especially a bride wearing a fancy dress." He scanned the trail, barely wide enough for two horses side by side. "I guess we could clear the path out a little more so that a horse and buggy could fit through, but still…it'd be a tight fit, and we'd lose some of the trees in the process."

Her eyes dimmed with his words, and John realized that while he was a dreamer, he also had enough realism to his nature to know when something wouldn't work. She, on the other hand, saw this cup as half full.

"Yeah, you're probably right."

Unfortunately, her sad response brought back memories of his own frustration when the bank told him that the dude ranch wouldn't work. "Then again, if someone wanted to have a wedding up here, we could make it work. I'm not about to tell a guest no. The customer is always right in business, right?"

The light returned to those bright blue eyes, and she smiled. "You don't have to humor me. I know it'd be difficult and a little odd, but when I see a pretty location, I automatically start thinking of weddings."

John shouldn't ask. He knew he shouldn't. But he'd never been one to hold back from asking something if he wanted to know the answer. "You engaged or something?"

"Engaged? Oh, no," she said, shaking her head. "Definitely not. I just— Well, all girls my age think about weddings, you know?" Her face flushed a little with the admission.

"I didn't know, but I do now." And inside, he was glad Miss Brooks wasn't spoken for. Even if she'd head back where she came from in a month, he was happy there wasn't some suit-wearing guy with a truckload of money waiting in Chicago for her return. And he wasn't going to analyze why he felt so pleased about that.

She cleared her throat, looked away from John and back to the abundance of color lining the path. "So, what do you think about having some photos taken of the trees now, while they're in bloom, to show on the site?"

He knew she'd intentionally changed the subject, but he didn't mind. He wasn't all that comfortable talking about weddings and engagements, either. Besides, he'd gotten the information he wanted; Dana wasn't planning a wedding of her own in the near future. "I've already taken some photos with my phone," he said, "but I've talked with Mandy Brantley, who owns the photography studio in the town square, about taking professional photos for the site. She's supposed to come out this week. She'll send the pictures to my younger brother, Casey. He's designing the website for us for free. He's young, but he's talented."

She seemed to think about his answer, then she tilted her head and continued surveying the magnificent blooms. "I can get some of our advertising and web specialists to help with the site. They've done beautiful work and would be happy to help with this project. We could even send one of our photographers down here to take the photos, if you like."

John hadn't thought to ask her opinion about designing the website and taking the pictures. If she was investing in his dude ranch—and she was the sole investor willing to gamble on his dream—he should let her have more control. Dana had an abundance of assets at her fingertips, highly paid, experienced advertising specialists and web designers. And they would all come running if she asked them to head this way.

On the other hand, when John needed something done, he turned to family and friends, people with less experience, but people who cared about him and would typically do the work for free. Dana was used to having the best and paying for the best. Mandy had been so excited about taking the photos, and Casey was thrilled about the opportunity to design the site. But what if Dana wouldn't be satisfied with the final product? "Would you rather someone from Brooks International take the photos and design the site?"

She turned her attention from the blooms back to John, and he braced himself for her response. He'd started to believe that she enjoyed and even appreciated the ranch, but if the people of Claremont weren't good enough for a project backed by Brooks International, then she was no different than MaciJo, saying that it wasn't possible to "be anything" in this tiny town. Mandy Brantley might not be a world-renowned photographer, but she'd won awards at the state level, and John knew she'd do a good job photographing the ranch. And Casey had only recently started working with web designs, but he knew and loved the ranch, and John believed that personal touch would be conveyed in his design.

Dana cleared her throat, her eyes softening as she shook her head. "I'm so sorry. I didn't mean that I thought Mandy and Casey wouldn't do a great job. I think they'll do an incredible job, especially since they know this area so well. The guys in Chicago would be hard-pressed to put a ranch feel to their work." She shrugged. "They deal mostly in marketing overpriced real estate. All I meant was that if Casey wants some help with descriptions or with how to make something on the site work the way he wants, I do have the resources to help him get it the way he wants it. And if Mandy needs any help manipulating photos, we have people for that, as well. But I want Casey to design the site and Mandy to take the photos, because that's what you want, and this is *your* business."

John's relief was instant. "They'll do a great job. I'm sure of it."

"I don't doubt that. You want potential guests to really feel the place, to sense everything that I'm experiencing today on these trails. The best people to convey that are those who have lived around it, like Casey and Mandy. There probably isn't a single person at Brooks International who has ever stepped foot on a farm, much less ridden a horse or hiked a trail. Except me, of course."

John's smile came easily. "I'm a little defensive when it comes to people and things I care about. Mandy and Casey are both pretty excited about helping."

"I'm excited about their helping us, too." She stroked

Fallon's mane but continued looking at John. "It's a rare thing, though, to see someone who would be loyal to his friends when he has a chance at something that might be perceived as better. That's not the way things work in Chicago, not the way things usually work in business."

John could only state the truth. "Well, that's the way we do things down here. We're loyal, and we take care of our own." He thought of MaciJo, turning her back on John when she had a chance at a "better" life. "Most of us around here, anyway. That's the way I was raised, and it's pretty much the only way I know."

She smiled, and at the same moment, those golden rays of sun pushed through the trees to cast her in a glistening spotlight once more. "I could get used to that, to loyalty and people who take care of their own. Honest to a fault, that's how my father would've described it."

"Nothing wrong with being honest." He moved Red closer to Fallon.

"I'd better not get too used to it, though, or I might not be able to adjust to the cutthroat business tactics of Chicago when I go back."

"Maybe you'll find out you want to stay down here." John had no idea what made him make the bold statement, but he couldn't deny the whisper in his heart saying that's exactly what he wanted—for Dana to stay—at least a little longer than a month. She'd only been here a couple of days and already he didn't want to think about her leaving.

Luckily, she didn't take the comment too seriously. She laughed, a rich, throaty laugh that made him grin. "Yeah, I can just hear Ryan if I told him I'd stay in Ala-

bama and live on a farm." She took Fallon closer to one
of the lower branches, plucked a hot-pink bloom from
the limb and put it behind her ear. "How does it look?"

The vivid hue accented her cheeks and somehow
made her eyes an even brighter shade of blue. The image
of Dana on Fallon with the rhododendrons surrounding
her silhouette was breathtaking.

"Stay right there." He fished his phone from his
pocket, activated the camera and snapped her picture.
Glancing at the image on his display, the bold colors
surrounding the stunning woman bathed in golden
spears of sunlight, he didn't hold back his thoughts.
"Beautiful."

Her cheeks flushed from his compliment. Then, obviously embarrassed, she turned Fallon away and looked
ahead. "So where does this trail lead?"

He loved how sensitive she was to compliments.
She wasn't conceited about her beauty and presumably didn't even realize the effect she had on him. But
she *was* affecting him, with every word, every move.
Right now, with her cheeks tinged pink as she awaited
his answer, all John wanted to do was brush his fingertips across her cheeks.

He cleared his throat and cleared his head of the ir-
rational thought. This was Dana Brooks, a millionaire
businesswoman from Chicago, and she was here because of her investment, not because of John. In four
weeks, she'd return to Chicago, and only a fool would
let himself fall for a woman destined to leave.

He moved past her on Red. "Now, I can't tell you
where the trail leads. When I take the ranch guests for

rides, I'll want them to be surprised at what we find along the trails. If I tell you everything, you won't experience the same effect."

"Oh, right." She laughed, looking adorable with the hot-pink flower tucked behind her ear. "So there's more to see on this trail? More than a colorful rainbow of rhododendron blooms?"

He was glad she couldn't detect how hard he was trying to rein in his emotions. Surely she wasn't feeling anything like that toward him, not toward an Alabama rancher. He needed to stay focused on the task at hand, showing her this trail. "Come on, I'll show you. And I've still got to tell you the background of dude ranches. That's also part of this tour." He led Red along the trail, the gelding's hooves crunching against the fallen leaves and pine straw covering the path.

"So this is a tour now?" Her amusement with his attempt to play tour guide made him grin. She really was a lot of fun.

"Yes, it's a tour. The nickel tour."

"I didn't pay a nickel—" she tapped her jeans "—and the only thing in my pocket is a phone, so you're out of luck. I'm only in this for the free tour."

"No, you didn't pay, but those ranch guests are going to pay for their stay, so I want it to be worth their while. And since I'm feeling generous, I'll give you the nickel tour for free."

Another small laugh bubbled out, and she said, "Okay, tell me a dude ranch story."

"Sorry, ma'am. This isn't the time for the dude ranch

story. This is the time for us to see the next picturesque scene along our path up Lookout Mountain."

"Picturesque. Good description, cowboy."

He was exhausted from lack of sleep, and shouldn't be having this much fun chatting on a horse ride this afternoon. He should be home sleeping and getting ready for tonight's shift at the steel plant. But he couldn't think of anywhere else he wanted to be, especially with her seemingly flirting with him. Dana Brooks, *the* Dana Brooks, *flirting* with him. "Thanks, I've got a few five-dollar words in my pocket."

She clicked the roof of her mouth and urged along Fallon, who'd stopped to look at a squirrel. "So I get a five-dollar word on my nickel tour."

He smiled. "You see? You're getting your money's worth already."

They continued the teasing banter as they moved beyond the scent of the rhododendrons; then the crisp scents of pine, damp earth and woods claimed dominion once more. The quiet sounds of the woods—breezes filtering through the trees, birds chirping, owls hooting—enveloped them as they moved farther along the trail.

Dana sighed. "I can't get over how peaceful it is here, as if we've removed ourselves from the outside world. My phone hasn't gone off at all since we started on the trail."

"I've got an answer for that. I'm sure you don't have a signal. No phones catch a signal up here. Nice, isn't it?"

She laughed. "Yes, it is. And I'll bet Ryan is ready to kill me for not responding to his texts."

John had never met her brother, of course, but he'd

seen his pictures online. Ryan Brooks looked as if he was in his late twenties or early thirties. No way should he be as stiff as the guy Dana kept describing. "It's Saturday. Shouldn't he be taking the day off?"

"He should, but he won't. I'm sure he's been in his home office all day finalizing details for our latest deal."

"Which is…"

"Buying a golf resort in Miami. It was my project initially, but Ryan took it over when Daddy got sick."

John heard what she didn't say. "When you stopped working to stay with your dad and take care of him, you mean."

She nodded, and just like that, all the flirty teasing disappeared, and he saw hints of sadness in her eyes.

"And now Ryan wants you back in control, working with him on the same kind of deals you handled before you left to take care of your dad." John guided Red down the path, but he wasn't paying as much attention to his surroundings anymore. Instead, he studied the myriad of emotions playing on Dana's face. Why *had* she left Chicago and projects that she'd started—big projects evidently—to help him start a dude ranch in Alabama? It didn't make sense to him, even if he was glad she was here, and he assumed it didn't make sense to her brother, either.

"Is that a waterfall?" Dana's question brought his attention back to the trail and the next sight he planned to show her along the way.

John decided to put off any intense discussions regarding what brought the pretty millionaire to his ranch in Alabama. Instead, he wanted to enjoy the moment with the woman who captivated him with her genuine appreciation for the ranch's beauty. "That's our next stop, and where I plan to set up camp with our guests."

They rounded the next bend in the trail and viewed a scene that rivaled that of the rhododendrons in distinctive beauty. Jasper Falls tumbled into a babbling creek that flowed along the mountain. From this vantage point, Dana could see the falls, the creek and the woods dotted with white dogwood trees. "I need to have this graded a bit more, so we'll have more room for tents and we'll need a small building for supplies, but guests will set up camp here, by the creek, so they can swim, tube, that kind of thing. And if you look behind the falls, there is a recessed area where they can actually hike behind the water."

"So can we hike behind the water? Now?" Her excitement bristled through her words. Then she glanced at her watch. "Or do we need to get back? You still haven't slept, and I'm sure you weren't planning to stay out here all afternoon. We can come back another day."

His eyes were beginning to droop a bit from lack of sleep, but there was no way he'd leave now. He could see how much she wanted to go behind the falls, and it was an incredible experience. Sleep could wait. This was more important. And he knew how much sleep he needed to be fine for work. He had time, and he'd spend it with Dana. "I'm fine. Let's tie up the horses here, and I'll show you the back side of the falls."

Her smile claimed her face. "You sure?"

As if he could tell her no, with the way her face lit up and her eyes danced. "I'm sure."

They let the horses drink their fill of the cool creek water, then left them tied near the creek's bank while they ventured toward the falls.

"I love the mist from a waterfall." She paused as they moved toward the tumbling water and closed her eyes to let the cold vapor caress her face.

John found the mist refreshing, too, but not as refreshing as watching Dana lose herself in the feel of it against her skin. He swallowed thickly, turned his attention from the pretty lady to the falls. He was tired, and his judgment felt a little off as a result, because this tour suddenly felt more intimate than he'd intended. Which was crazy, he knew. He'd come to know Dana very well over the past few months, as a business investor. Maybe because of all those chats, he felt closer to her now than someone he'd only met in person yesterday.

Surely that was it.

"This way?" she asked, moving ahead of him and following the stone path that led behind the falls. Her hair was growing damp from the mist, and she pushed it away from her face.

John loved it that she didn't care if her hair was wet or that the path wasn't all that easy, formed by large, somewhat jagged rocks that required a bit of agility to make your way through. "Yes, but let me lead." He stepped past her on a large boulder. "Hold my hand."

She visibly swallowed, then slid her hand into his. Their eyes met, and John was once again taken by the intimacy of the location and the moment and the woman whose hand trembled slightly within his.

"Stay with me. The rocks are slippery in spots, but I won't let you fall. Step where I do, okay?"

Her face glistened from the spray of the falls. "I'm ready."

John followed the path he'd taken many times before, stepping on the bigger, sturdier stones and steering clear of the slick, flat areas that might send them both toppling.

They reached the center of the falls and he stopped, turned to see Dana, her eyes blinking through the spray and her smile mesmerizing.

"I've seen so many waterfalls before," she said, a giggle trickling through her words, "but I've never been behind one like this!" She shifted on the rock to take in the panoramic view, the curtain of water enclosing them within the mountain. The movement caused her foot to slip, and her hand tightened within his as she lost her balance. "Oh!"

John felt her begin to slide away. Instinct took over and he quickly moved to catch her before she tumbled. So instead of hitting the wet, jagged rocks, Dana fell against him.

Her fragrance was sweeter than the rhododendrons. And John knew he should let her go, but instead he held her for a moment too long.

"You said you wouldn't let me fall," she whispered. "And you didn't."

"No, I didn't." But John wasn't so certain he could keep himself from falling—hard—for Dana Brooks.

Chapter Six

"Ryan, I didn't have a signal, so I *couldn't* answer you." Dana covered the phone and whispered to Eden, Georgiana and Abi, "You go on inside. I'll come in as soon as I finish talking to my brother."

Abi huffed out a disappointed, "Awww," but Eden, smiling, steered her granddaughter into the clothing store on the charming Claremont town square. Dana hadn't been able to truly appreciate the quaintness of the place yet, however, because Ryan called as they were parking the car, and he hadn't stopped talking— and complaining—yet.

"I approved the Miami press release without you. It couldn't wait. The media down there, including CNN, had already caught wind of it, and our PR folks didn't want to miss the opportunity. You'd think since that was your baby, you'd have been interested in the announcement."

"We were on the mountain, and cell phones don't pick up a signal there." Her mind drifted back to the beauty of the trail, the waterfall and, more than that, the delight she'd experienced in John's arms. She hadn't imagined the look he'd given her, as if he wanted to kiss her behind that cascading water.

"No signal. That's ridiculous, Dana. Do you really think any kind of a business, even a dude ranch, could survive in a place so far behind? You know, when I searched for information on Claremont, I ran across this joke about Alabama. Reminds me of what you're saying about the cell signals, or lack thereof."

Dana didn't want to hear the joke, so she didn't ask. Unfortunately, that didn't keep him from telling her.

"When you cross the state line leading into Alabama, do you know what the sign reads?"

She eyed the pretty clothes in the shopwindow and didn't respond.

"Welcome to Alabama. Set your watch back six years." His laughter cackled into the phone. "Did you hear me?"

"I heard."

"Come back where you belong, Dana. Dad didn't want…"

"No, Ryan." She wouldn't listen to him say it again, "He *did* want us to help people starting out. And Daddy moved to Chicago from Jackson, Mississippi. He was born not far from where I am now, and he built a Fortune 500 company from the ground up. How do you know John's business won't be just as successful?"

"John? So you're on a first-name basis with the rancher now? Is *that* what this is about? You've got some kind of crush on the country boy from the sticks?"

A woman passed by Dana on the sidewalk and held up her hand in a wave. Dana didn't know the lady, of course, but she held a hand up, too. She waited until the lady was farther away before responding to her brother. "No, that's not what this is about. It's about helping someone achieve his dreams, the way Dad achieved his. It's about helping others—period."

"You do remember that you agreed to drop the whole rags-to-riches idea if this dude ranch doesn't make it, right?" She heard a computer keyboard clicking over the line, Ryan unwilling to stop working even while he talked to her on the phone.

"The dude ranch will make it." Dana hoped that was true. So far she'd only viewed the property and heard John's ideas, which were good, but they'd have to get into all the specifics regarding ranch legalities soon— as in no later than Monday. Four weeks wasn't a lot of time for her to prove to Ryan and the Brooks International board that the dude ranch could hold its own. But she could do it. She had to.

"If you say so. I'm more inclined to think this cowboy crush may be more of what has you in Alabama than investing in his off-the-wall dude ranch. And speaking of crushes, William Montgomery has called the office repeatedly, asking if I've heard from you. He said he left you two messages about the gala at the Art Institute next month."

Abi waved at Dana through the shopwindow. Dana waved back, eager to get this call over with and shop with her new friends. "I saw one text from William. Must have missed the other one."

"And you didn't respond, I take it? You *are* still representing Brooks International at the event, aren't you? They're officially opening the Lawrence Brooks wing and want a family representative there for the event. Dad is getting recognition for his lifetime of support to the Art Institute, and he'd have wanted one of us there for this. And you know I'm already slated to be in California that week. We told them you'd do the honors. They're expecting you. Plus, William wants to spend time with you. In my opinion, he's ready to make this relationship something permanent, and you know Dad wanted the two of you together."

"Dad liked William, but he never said anything about wanting us to end up together. In fact, I told Daddy that I enjoy attending corporate functions with William, but I don't feel *that way* about him." She'd never felt nearly as much for William Montgomery in the three or so years they'd casually dated as she experienced in one afternoon with John. The few times she and William had kissed had been cold and somewhat forced. The afternoon she'd spent with John warmed her to her toes.

"So you disappointed Dad about William, too? He planned on you two marrying, whether you realize it or not. And William's company is solid, he isn't dating you for your name, or your money. Bet you can't say that about your Alabama rancher."

"I'm not dating John." Though she was definitely thinking about the possibility. In any case, she had tolerated as much as she could from Ryan now. She knew he didn't like handling the brunt of the company decisions on his own, but he had a capable board and plenty of high-priced advisers at his disposal. And he'd never complained when she'd been away for months taking care of their father. But because he wasn't happy with her decision to invest in potential entrepreneurs with money from Brooks International, he'd been adamant—and rude—about expressing his opinions. And she'd heard enough. "I have to go, Ryan. I'm shopping."

"Shopping? In Claremont, Alabama? The information I found online today put the population at 4,500." He laughed. "So where is there to shop in Nowhere, Alabama?"

She looked up to see the name of the store Georgiana, Eden and Abi had entered, and then she smiled. "Consigning Women."

His gasp echoed through the line. "A consignment shop? You? Are you serious?"

"Goodbye, Ryan." She disconnected and then, for good measure, turned off her phone and dropped it in her purse. "What do you know? I just lost my signal."

Abi poked her head out the door of the shop. "Are you coming, Miss Dana? I've already matched some pretty things for Mommy, but I saw a dress for you, too. It's blue, like your eyes. You can wear it to church tomorrow, if you buy it. And we'll get you some clothes for the farm, too, so you won't have to keep wearing Mommy's stuff."

"But it's fine for you to wear my things if you want," Georgiana called from within the store.

Dana had never been in a consignment shop. For that matter, she'd never been to an honest-to-goodness town square. And she was excited about both. Stepping across the threshold, she heard contemporary Christian music, not at all what she usually heard while shopping, but the lyrics—about hanging on to God and casting away her worries—lifted her spirits after the frustrating phone call with Ryan.

"This is our favorite store ever!" Abi pulled a pink hat with a red flower embellishment off a wall hook and shoved it on top of her curls. "How's this look?"

Dana immediately thought of this afternoon, when she put the bright pink rhododendron behind her ear and asked John the same question. He'd said she looked beautiful. Her pulse skittered at the memory.

Abi raised her brows waiting for Dana's answer.

"It's very pretty. Beautiful."

The little girl nodded. "Yep, it is." She pulled it off, and a few wild red strands stuck up from her head as though reaching to get back into the hat. Abi gazed at the price noted on the brim. "Miss Maribeth, is this just a dollar?"

A petite woman who looked a little younger than Dana stepped from behind a rack of colorful scarves, an orange ribbon threaded through the thick brunette braid hanging past her right shoulder. "Yes, and it looks wonderful on you." She wore a multicolored print dress with splashes of orange, red and royal blue. Her red satin pumps matched the outfit perfectly, as did her earrings and multicolored bangles. She looked from Abi to Dana. "Is this who you were telling me about, Abi?"

"Yep, she's the one. She came all the way from a windy town to come down here and help Uncle John with our dude ranch. We don't have the dude ranch yet, but we're fixing it up and stuff, and when it's done, we'll go camping a lot, and I'll probably need to teach all the little kids about horse riding, so I'm taking extra lessons."

Dana extended a hand and a smile. "Hi, I'm Dana Brooks."

"I'm Maribeth Walton. Pleasure to meet you." She shook Dana's hand. "And I know who you are. You're one of my best models."

"Really?" Abi's brows shot up a notch. "She's on the wall? Where?"

"I've seen Dana on the wall in here," Eden called from farther back in the store.

"I haven't," Georgiana said, then laughed at her own joke.

"On the wall?" Dana asked.

"Come on, I'll show you." Maribeth motioned for Dana to follow her through the store. Stunning outfits, complete with shoes and accessories, hung from the ceiling and along every wall. The circular rack assemblies on the floor were well-organized, color-coordinated and labeled not only by size but also by "look."

Dana stopped at a rack that showcased a gray pastel dress with turquoise accents around the neck and sleeves. Gray suede pumps dangled from a hook nearby, as did turquoise earrings and bracelets. "Oh, my. This is incredible."

"Oh, thanks! That's one of my favorites, too. It's the outfit Kate Middleton wore to the London premiere of *African Cats* last year."

"It's…what?" Dana looked at the dress in a whole new light. Surely this tiny consignment shop in Claremont, Alabama, hadn't scored a dress worn by royalty.

Maribeth laughed. "Not the real one, of course." She pointed to a photo hanging from a ribbon tied to the rack beside the outfit. Sure enough, the picture displayed the Duchess of Cambridge wearing a dress remarkably similar to the one Maribeth had on sale for—Dana peeked at the tag—merely $25. "This is what I do. I study fashion and then try to mimic the styles in the photo with items that have been brought in for consignment. The customers like knowing they're wearing something similar to the stars for a price they can afford in Claremont."

"That's brilliant." Dana, beyond impressed, looked at the next outfit, a cuffed white blazer with black cropped jeans and cap-toed pumps. She flipped the photo hanging from a black satin ribbon. "Gwyneth Paltrow."

Maribeth nodded. "She's one of my favorites."

"I love this." Dana ran a hand down the blazer.

"The whole outfit is less than $40," Maribeth said, "and that includes the shoes. Of course, the drawback is that each outfit is unique based on what's been turned in for consignment, so if the items aren't your size, I don't have more in the back." She shrugged. "But, in my opinion, that's part of what makes the shopping experience fun. You know that whatever you get is more than likely unique for you."

"Unique for you in Claremont," Georgiana said, holding Eden's forearm as they made their way from the back of the store toward the center, where Dana, Abi and Maribeth admired the stylish selections. "They're one-of-a-kind looks here," Georgiana continued, "but obviously, the looks have been seen before on movie stars and princesses."

"What a terrific idea," Dana said. "You said something about my being on your wall? What wall?"

"This one." Maribeth pointed to a large wall to the right of the checkout counter. Fashion photographs of celebrities and models covered the entire span of space like a gigantic fashionista collage. "These are some of my favorite looks and the ones I am most often asked to re-create for my customers. And here you are." She pointed to a photo of Dana at the Tribeca Film Festival. William had escorted her to the event, but he'd been cropped out of the picture that had made its way to one of the weekly tabloids. That'd been Dana's first time to go out after her father's death, and the press was hungry for a photo of the new heiress. Beside the picture, Maribeth had attached a white note with pink script writing. *Cocktail dress with illusion neckline, colorful Bulgari jewelry and patent leather Jimmy Choos. Find Dana Brooks's look in our Night on the Town section.* Dana saw at least three more of her photos merged with all the others.

"That is so cool that you're one of the people on the wall, Miss Dana! I can't wait to tell Uncle John!"

Dana felt her cheeks heat, a little embarrassed that she was included on the "wall" with celebrities, several of whom were acquaintances. The collage made her feel oddly separate and apart from the sweet people around her, and she didn't know what to say.

Maribeth put a hand on Dana's shoulder. "I hope you

see it as an honor and aren't offended that I put your pictures up, but I do love those outfits. I've been able to re-create them a couple of times, though I don't have all the necessary pieces right now for a complete ensemble." She smiled. "But you aren't looking for those kinds of clothes to wear around here, anyway, are you? Abi said you needed some things for the farm. I have separates on sale, too, at the back of the store. We'll get you all set."

"Thank you." Dana had personal stylists to help create the right look for various occasions, but she was more curious about what Maribeth picked out than she'd been to see the outfits put together by any of her high-priced stylists. From the look of the outfits around the store, Maribeth Walton had more style than all of them combined.

"And she needs that blue dress I saw, remember?" Abi grabbed Dana's hand. "Come here, and I'll show you. It'll be a good one for church tomorrow. You are coming to church with us, aren't you? Uncle John goes, even after he has to work all night, 'cause he says it's the best way to start the day. Then he takes a nap, 'cause he's sleepy, but he'll go to church first."

Dana knew he hadn't gotten enough rest today, because he'd spent the afternoon taking her on a trail ride. He had gone back to his cabin to sleep when she, Georgiana, Eden and Abi had left for the town square. Strange, that she had only spent a little over a day with him in person, yet she missed him now.

"See, this is it? Won't it be pretty for church?" Abi tugged at the blue print dress.

"That's modeled after the one Cameron Diaz wore to some movie premiere," Maribeth said. "But I love that dress, so feminine and light. The tri-strand of pearls and the pearl stud earrings really pick up the white floral print on the fabric, don't you think?"

"It's lovely, Abi." Dana touched the soft material. "And I do think I'd like to wear this to church tomorrow." She checked the tag. "And the size is right, too."

Abi clapped her hands together. "Great!"

Georgiana smiled. "Okay, Abi, now that she's bought what you picked out, we should probably let her get what she needs. Maribeth, can you find Dana some clothes for the farm?"

"Sure."

Dana followed Maribeth to the area for separates and quickly learned that the savvy stylist could also select clothing quickly. Within twenty minutes, Dana had plenty of farm clothes—cute ensembles of Western shirts and jeans, as well as mud boots and work gloves. Granted, her mud boots were stylishly pink, as were the cowboy boots she'd selected, but they were still suitable for the farm, according to her fellow shoppers.

"So, you're helping John start a dude ranch?" Maribeth asked as she rang up Dana's purchases.

"It's an investment for our company, and the first one we've ever done like this, with a start-up business. I'm really hoping that I can get the board to agree to invest in more future entrepreneurs like John."

Maribeth's hands paused on the old-fashioned cash register, her brown eyes studying Dana. But then she turned her focus to Eden and Georgiana and asked,

"How's John doing? Still working himself to death? Still hardly dating?" Maribeth's glance darted Dana's way with the last question.

"He's been very busy with work," Georgiana said.

Dana wondered if the pretty brunette had an interest in Georgiana's handsome brother-in-law, too.

Maribeth continued with the purchase and then announced that Dana's total was just shy of $300. Dana couldn't believe the number of items she'd purchased for that small amount.

"Really?" she asked.

"Is that too much?" Abi held the pink flower-embellished hat that Eden had already purchased for her granddaughter.

Dana grinned at the precious little girl. "No, sweetie. I just meant that it's really nice to get so many pretty clothes for that price."

"So you don't have to put the blue dress back or anything, do you?"

Dana suspected that the Cutters had put things back before, and the thought of it broke her heart. "No, honey, I don't."

"That's good, 'cause I think Uncle John is going to really like that blue dress." She put the pink hat on and then moved toward the front of the store. "I'm going to see if Nelson's is still open. They keep the milk-shake sign lit up if they're making shakes. You've got to get a double-chocolate milk shake. It's the best."

"Okay." Dana waited for Abi to get out of earshot and then looked to the other women to see if anyone else thought it odd that Abi said John would like the blue dress.

Eden and Maribeth were both looking at Dana, and Georgiana smiled a little too brightly.

"Abi saw you and John riding back across the field after your trail ride and said she thinks you should be her uncle's girlfriend," Georgiana explained. "I hope her remark didn't embarrass you, but apparently she has it in her head that the blue dress is all it will take for you to become his girlfriend."

Dana swallowed. "Oh." She knew the statement warranted more of a response, but she didn't have anything to offer.

Maribeth leaned forward against the counter. "Well, I'll tell you what, it's been years since he was serious with anyone, all because of MaciJo Riley taking his heart and stomping on it. And I never saw them as right together, anyway. She always wanted something better than what she had, used to come in here and turn her nose up at my outfits because they didn't have the labels or prices of the real things."

"But they honestly look just as good," Dana said, not knowing anything about this MaciJo person but instantly developing a dislike for the woman who'd hurt John.

Maribeth's brown eyes sparkled. "Another reason I like you, and the fact that you know a good-looking outfit when you see it. You're even on my wall. MaciJo sure isn't."

Georgiana and Eden laughed at that.

Dana grinned. "Thanks."

"I've always said the same thing about John Cutter. And it isn't because I'm trying to get him for myself or anything. We've been friends forever, and I just don't think God's sent me the right man yet. I figure I'll know when I meet him."

"You will," Georgiana assured, obviously thinking of Landon.

Eden placed her hand on top of her daughter's on the counter. "I'm so glad you and Landon found each other, dear."

"Well, God will give me my right one eventually," Maribeth continued, "but even so, I've always said the same thing about John Cutter."

"What's that?" Eden asked.

"That a guy who looks that good—and acts that good—shouldn't be wasted on tending to livestock. He deserves to love and be loved well."

Eden nodded.

Georgiana smirked. "Well said, Maribeth."

Dana didn't voice her response, but inside, her heart whispered, *"Let it be me."*

Chapter Seven

John rarely overslept, but he hadn't wanted his dream to end. In the dream, he hadn't merely thought about kissing Dana behind the waterfall; he had. Yesterday, in reality, after catching her to keep her from falling, he'd stepped away and attempted to joke about her stumbling. Then he'd led her back to the horses and claimed he needed to get back to the cabin to sleep.

He'd need to get a grip on this attraction if they were going to maintain a business relationship—the only type of relationship they could have if she was leaving in four weeks.

Red waited beside the cabin as though knowing it was Sunday and John would need a ride to his truck. Within minutes, they began crossing the field toward the house. He assumed the rest of the family—and presumably Dana—had already headed to church, and he hated that he missed the chance to escort her, introduce her to Brother Henry and everyone else during her first visit. It was hard enough last night knowing she went to the town square for the first time without him. He'd wanted to see her face when she saw the three-tiered fountain at the center of the square, the huge oak trees on both sides of the fountain, the brick storefronts topped with decorative eaves.

He suspected there weren't that many things the city girl hadn't seen and experienced in her life, but Claremont seemed to hold an abundance. John wanted to be the one to show it all to Dana. But more than anything else, he'd wanted to take her to church. The people at Claremont Community Church were like his second family, especially after the way they embraced him when his mother died. He'd felt so alone with Landon overseas and Casey merely a kid, a kid who had suddenly become John's responsibility. The church folks had been there when John needed help back then, and nowadays he looked forward to seeing them each week. Today he was even more anxious to see them, because he'd planned to introduce them to Dana.

But, because he was a good ten minutes late, she would've already caught a ride with Georgiana, Landon and Abi. He crested the final hill that led to the house, looked toward the log cabin and immediately caught a glimpse of pale blue on the porch. Then the sunlight caught white-blond hair and, unless he was seeing things, highlighted her smile as she saw him approach.

She lifted a hand and moved her fingers in a feminine wave that did strange things to his pulse. John nodded in return and guided Red to the barn, dismounted and walked toward the house, as though he wasn't thrilled she had stayed behind, presumably waiting for him to accompany her to church.

She started down the porch steps, the soft fabric of the skirt shifting gently as she moved, and her pretty legs embellished by an adorable pair of cowboy boots. "Now that's something you don't see every day," she said.

John swallowed. Have mercy, she was cute. And beautiful. And so way out of his league. "What's that?"

"A guy riding up on a horse to go to church."

He grinned, a little more at ease with the stunning woman walking toward him now. "Maybe *you* don't see it every day in Chicago. Folks around here see it every Sunday."

She glanced down at her dress. "But you do take the truck to the church, right? I don't think I'm dressed quite right for horseback riding."

He personally thought she'd look absolutely perfect riding sidesaddle in the blue dress, but he kept that thought to himself. "Yeah, Red's good to get to the main house, but we'd never make it to church on time riding him the whole way. And we're late as it is." He nodded toward the truck. "You want a ride?"

"I suppose I do—" she laughed "—because if you don't take me, I'll be hard-pressed to get there since they didn't bring my new rental yet."

With everything that had happened yesterday, he'd forgotten about her vehicle. "I'll call the rental place today and see what happened."

"I already did. They weren't able to get another one until at least Monday. I told them I'd be okay, since all of you have been so gracious to let me use your vehicles or drive me if I need to go anywhere." One corner of her mouth lifted. "That's assuming you're still willing to give me a ride to church."

He chuckled. "Of course. And I can't imagine a reason you'll need that SUV, anyway. Most of the time, we'll stay at the farm. And if you need to go anywhere we can take you or, as you said, you can use one of our vehicles. Why don't you cancel the rental?" If she didn't have her own car, she'd have to rely on him a bit more. And he liked that, almost as much as he liked the thought of her riding around next to him in the old blue truck. "So, what do you say? Cancel the rental?"

"Sure."

He opened the passenger door. "I'll call and cancel it for you." He glanced at her feet. "Nice boots."

"Abi picked everything out at the store last night. They weren't originally paired with the dress, but Maribeth thought they added Southern charm."

"Maribeth likes clothes. She was always dressing up in high school, not like Sunday dressing up, but different than every other girl there, that's for sure."

"She's talented. I've never seen anything like her store before." Dana moved near him as she climbed in, and he caught a whiff of something sweet. He must've audibly inhaled, because she laughed. "You like that smell?"

Caught. "Yeah, I do."

"It's one of Georgiana's body lotions. I brought some lotions and perfumes with me from home, but Abi wanted me to try this one today."

He laughed. "*That's* why it seemed familiar. I took Abi Christmas shopping last year, and she wanted my opinion on a gift for her mom. She knew Georgiana loved body lotion, but she couldn't decide on a scent."

"So *you* picked one for her?" The look on Dana's face said she couldn't see John selecting a lotion. He certainly would never have volunteered for the job if Abi hadn't asked him to go.

"Picking it out was easy. Going into that girly Scents and Sensibility store on the square with half of Claremont there Christmas shopping, now *that* was hard." He started the truck, while Dana giggled from the passenger's seat.

"Why didn't she get Landon to take her?"

"She said she didn't want him knowing what she was getting her mom."

"And why not Eden?"

"I suggested that, but Abi wanted me to take her for some reason." He caught Dana's knowing look. "Yeah, I was set up. She knew I'd cave when she asked to also go to the Treasure Box, the Sweet Stop *and* Nelson's."

"And you bought her something at every store, I take it?" Another small laugh followed the question.

"I can't tell her no." He shrugged. "It's a weakness."

"You'd better watch yourself when she turns sixteen and asks to go car shopping."

He grinned, thinking about his adorable niece. "At least I've got a few years to build up my resistance."

"Personally, I don't know how anyone would turn down a trip to Nelson's. I've had a lot of milk shakes, but nothing like that double-chocolate one I had last night."

"Ah, so she got y'all to take her to Nelson's? I guess I'm not the only one who can't say no to Abi. Did she hit you up for the Tiny Tots Treasure Box, too?"

Dana laughed. "Yes, but she didn't ask for anything in the toy store. We just went in and looked around because she said I needed to see how cool it was, and we skipped the candy shop since we knew we were going to have milk shakes."

He could almost see the group of females shopping in the square with Abi leading the pack and Dana taking it all in the same way she'd absorbed everything on the mountain yesterday. "So you enjoyed shopping in Claremont's tiny metropolis?"

"Every minute of it. The square is amazing, like something lifted out of the past, the geese squawking, the people shopping and visiting with each other as they meet. Everyone says hello or waves as though they know you—that's not like anything I'm used to. And then the kids everywhere, splashing and playing around the fountain, enjoying the gorgeous late afternoon and evening. I didn't want to leave."

He knew exactly what she meant, and he wished he'd have been there to see her experience it all, but he saw her excitement now, her appreciation for his town, and it touched his heart. He couldn't help that he missed her first visit to the square. He'd had to work, and that was that. At least he'd get to show her the church this morning.

They continued down the dirt driveway and, even

though the morning wasn't overly warm, the truck heated up quickly. Dana cranked her window down. The breeze blew her silky hair all over, and she gathered it the same way she had when they rode the Gator.

John cranked his window down, too. "Sorry, I ought to get the air fixed in this thing."

She squinted through the few strands of hair that escaped the makeshift ponytail and moved across her face with the gentle wind. "It isn't too warm. I just want to enjoy the breeze and the scents of the farm."

He laughed. "Some scents are a little strong at times. Might want to roll the window back up if you get a whiff of one of those, but we haven't fertilized recently, so you should be okay."

She held her wrist to her nose. "Speaking of scents, I can't remember what the lotion was called. I thought Abi told me…"

"Don't worry, I remember. It's called My Favorite Oatmeal Topping."

Her eyes grew wide. "Seriously?"

"Seriously. The store tries to give them all memorable Southern-sounding names. Needless to say, that one stuck with me. And they named it that because it smells like brown sugar, which is most folks' favorite oatmeal topping, at least around here."

"So, is that your favorite topping?"

"That, and raisins. And pecans. Sometimes apples. Every now and then grapes."

She smothered a laugh. "Can you even taste the oatmeal?"

"Barely, but it's good. You'll have to try it."

"Maybe I will." She sniffed her wrist again. "You're right, it does smell like brown sugar. I knew it was familiar but couldn't put my finger on it." They stopped at the end of the driveway, and she held her hand toward John. "So this is what you picked out?"

He already knew it was, but he took her hand in his, lifted her wrist and smelled the scent that he'd selected for Abi, as well as another underlying fragrance, feminine and sweet, purely Dana. "Yes, it is." He held her wrist a little longer, and looked up into blue eyes watching his every move. "It's a nice scent."

Her slender throat pulsed as she swallowed. "Yes, it is."

Releasing her hand was more difficult than it should have been, but John let go, and started toward the church.

They traveled at least a mile in a semi-awkward silence while he thought about the softness of her skin against his fingers.

Then Dana cleared her throat and asked, "Do you know what I realized last night?"

"No, what?"

"You said you would tell me about dude ranches yesterday, remember? You said that it was part of the nickel tour. But you never said anything about them." She ran her fingertips across the white flowers embroidered over the blue skirt. "I may have to ask for my nickel back."

"Last time I checked, you never gave me that nickel."

"Oh, right. I owe you." She shifted in the seat to

face him. "Will you tell the dude ranch story, anyway, Cowboy John?"

He liked the endearing nickname, thought he could get used to hearing her say it, too, truth be told. "Sure, Cowgirl Dana."

Her smile stretched to her cheeks. "Cowgirl Dana. Can't wait to share that with Ryan."

John had already determined from the few comments Dana had made about her brother that Ryan Brooks didn't want her here, didn't want Brooks International to invest in an Alabama rancher. Feeling as strongly as he did about family, John didn't like causing a rift between the siblings and hoped it was a friendly disagreement and nothing more. He also hoped that the dude ranch would be as successful as he planned, and Ryan would end up apologizing to his sister.

"So, tell me about dude ranches," she said. "And I promise I'll pay you that nickel."

He winked. "Okay, so here's the John Cutter short version on the history of dude ranches."

She straightened in the seat. "Go ahead, I'm all ears."

John cleared his throat and put on his best tour guide accent. "In the late 1800s, many East Coasters and Europeans were drawn to the simple lifestyle pioneers discovered out West." He noticed her head tilted, her eyes studying him with interest, and he realized he enjoyed sharing a bit of his knowledge with the savvy businesswoman. "The introduction of the transcontinental rail system provided easy travel from the East Coast to the Western frontier, and visitors began to come in droves. But in spite of the great expanse of the West, the travelers at the time outnumbered available accommodations."

She turned more toward John, rested her arm on the back of the seat and propped her chin on top of her hand as she listened.

"Consequently, cattle and horse ranchers were inundated with requests by friends and relatives to put them up, often for months. At first it was merely an exchange of hospitality, but soon the guests began offering money to their hosts, and that began the dude ranch. *Dude* happened to be a turn-of-the-century expression for strangers in a new land, and the term has stood the test of time."

She nodded. "I had never thought about where the term came from—that's so interesting. And your guests are going to love hearing the history."

He turned the truck into the church parking lot, pulled it under the shade of a Bradford pear tree, the white blossoms covering each branch like tufts of snow. "We're here."

She shifted her attention from John to the white-steepled church, towering magnolias and oak trees on each side, colorful flower beds filled with red tulips bordering the entrance and the remaining mature Bradford pears blooming stark white along the edge. "This could be a painting."

He grinned. "There's a local artist, Gina Brown, who is one of the church members here and owns the Gina Brown Art Gallery on the square. Her paintings of our church are some of her bestsellers."

"I can see why. And I remember seeing her gallery

at the square last night. I'll have to make a point to go inside the next time we go into town."

John liked hearing that *we* in her statement and looked forward to accompanying her to the square the next time she went. He climbed out of the truck, rounded the front and then opened her door. Her smile beamed back at him.

"I'm enjoying this day so much," she said.

"We've only ridden to church." But he knew what she meant, the closeness they shared, even when merely riding in a truck and chatting, was undeniable.

"I know, but this isn't the usual way I spend my Sundays, and I'm very happy about that." Before John could ask how she usually spent her Sundays, she continued. "The dude ranch story is fascinating. I can picture those people traveling across the country and needing a place to stay, especially after our trail ride yesterday. I think about them crossing mountains and fields like that, and I imagine that finding someone willing to house them along their journey was a real lifesaver."

"So you think that'll work for the nickel tour?"

"Oh, it's worth more than a nickel," she said. "I loved it, but more than that, I loved watching you tell it, as though you would've wanted to personally put those travelers up along their journey. I'm sure your guests will enjoy learning about it, too. You're going to do such a great job."

Her confidence touched his very soul. For years he'd dreamed of doing something that would allow him to achieve some measure of success. Now, with Dana's help, he saw the dream as a potential reality. "Thanks."

He looked toward the church. "Look, the doors are still open. We're not technically late until the greeters shut the doors." At that moment, Anna Bowman, an older woman who'd been friends with John's mother, stepped out and pulled one door closed.

"Looks like we'd better hurry, then." Dana stepped aside and grinned as he shut her door and took her hand.

"Looks like. Come on, let's go."

They sprinted across the parking lot, laughing as they made their way up the church steps and Anna stepped out to shut the other door. The sweet, silver-haired lady smiled. "John, did you work last night?"

"Yes, ma'am."

"But you never miss a Sunday service, do you?"

"The week wouldn't start right if I did." He nodded to Dana. "This is Dana Brooks. She's visiting us from Chicago."

"Well, it's wonderful to meet you, Dana. We're so glad you're visiting and glad you came to church this morning with John." She gave John and Dana the look that came over most older women around town whenever they saw John with a woman, the one that said they wondered—maybe even hoped—that there might be something to the pair.

Dana, her hand on her chest as she caught her breath from their sprint across the parking lot, didn't seem to notice. "Nice to meet you," she said.

"We're running a little late getting started," Anna explained. "Today's Mitch Gillespie's first day at church with the new baby, so they're doing the first Bible ceremony now." She looked to Dana. "We give a Bible to each baby on their first visit to church. Normally we give it to both parents, but Mitch's wife passed away right after the baby was born." She shook her head. "Very sad, but God has His reasons, right? And the church will be there for Mitch and his girls."

Dana's mouth flattened and she blinked a couple of times. "It's good that you'll be able to help him."

John knew she was probably thinking about her own mother's passing. He'd released her hand when they started up the stairs, but he reached for it and fastened her fingers through his. "Ready to go inside?"

"Oh, yes. Dear me, I'm blocking the door. Come on in." Anna stepped aside, and Dana and John entered just as the first song started.

Dana listened to the songs and the sermon, fighting tears. Probably because of the young widower in attendance, the entire service centered around Heaven and the joy waiting beyond this life. She thought about her father, twenty-six years ago. He'd been left with a newborn and a two-year-old when her own mother died giving birth to Dana. And then she thought about his death and how he'd found God right before he passed on.

The service ended, and Dana followed John out, nodding and smiling as he introduced her to each church member. But her thoughts remained on her father. He would've wanted her here, in this church, surrounded by people who believed, and finally feeling God's presence in her life. Her father would have been glad she was helping John achieve his dreams. He had wanted her to help others and forget about the lure of power and greed.

And at this moment in her life, Dana could honestly say she had no desire for power, no reason for greed. But she had a strong desire for faith and—she glanced at John—perhaps even love.

She knew she felt *something* for the down-to-earth, honest, hardworking and gorgeous cowboy. Before she came to Claremont, she'd have said she felt admiration for the rancher with the big dreams, endless optimism and charming wit. But now that she'd met John, she suspected that her admiration teetered on something more. And she could almost feel it each time she looked at the tall, fascinating cowboy.

By the time John finished introducing her to people and then showed her all the church activity boards along the lobby wall, the majority of the congregation had already left the building. Georgiana, Landon and Eden had followed Abi outside so she could play on the church's playground with her friends.

John seemed to wait until the line of church members visiting with the preacher had ended, then he steered her toward the white-haired man standing at the top of the stairs just outside the church. "Brother Henry, this is Dana Brooks."

Crinkle lines formed tiny starbursts around his eyes with his smile. "A pleasure to meet you, Ms. Brooks."

She shook the preacher's hand. "I enjoyed the lesson."

"Kind of hard not to enjoy a lesson about the glory

land, isn't it?" He gave her a soft smile. "God has given me great material to work with."

She nodded. "Yes, He has."

"So are you here visiting, or here to stay?"

"I'm visiting from Chicago."

"Dana is helping me with another business at the farm. She's investing in a dude ranch that I'm starting."

"You don't say. Well, now, you're investing, and you said you're from Chicago." Blue eyes focused on Dana. "Are you kin to Lawrence Brooks?"

She nodded. "My father."

"I've read all about his accomplishments, and heard about him on the news. I'm not all that hooked on the news typically. Too depressing the majority of the time. But I enjoy learning about people from the South who have done well, and your daddy, if I remember right, grew up on a cotton field in Mississippi, didn't he?"

"Yes, sir, he did."

"Then he moved up north and made a big name for himself in real estate." He tilted his head. "I read about him going on to his reward. I'm sorry for your loss."

She liked the way the preacher phrased it—*going on to his reward*. "Thank you."

"So have you seen much of Claremont yet? I imagine it's quite a contrast from your home, isn't it?"

"It is, but I'm really enjoying the difference."

"We went trail riding across Lookout Mountain yesterday," John said. "Saw Jasper Falls and the creek."

"Oh, that's beautiful up there." An elderly woman exited the church and moved to stand beside Brother Henry.

The preacher took her hand in his and smiled. "This is my wife, Mary. Mary, this is Dana Brooks. She's from Chicago and is helping the Cutter family start a dude ranch out at their farm."

"A dude ranch? What a great idea." The woman looked to John. "You know, you could include all the facts about horses from the Bible as part of what you share with your guests. I know I find it all interesting."

"Bible facts about horses?" John asked.

"Sure. I gathered a bunch of material that year we did the Vacation Bible School where the theme was Noah and the ark. We talked about animals in the Bible, so I researched the different animals to provide a few fun facts for the kids. Did you know there are over two hundred Bible verses about horses?"

"That's amazing," Dana said.

"I know." Mary smiled. "Might be something you can use on your dude ranch—the Bible information. I still have all those trivia questions and everything in the teacher supply room. I'll be happy to go get it for you, if you want."

"Nah, that's okay," John said. "We're going to head back to the ranch and get some lunch. But maybe another day."

"Yes, y'all can come look at it anytime that's convenient." Mary focused on Dana. "And are you planning to stay down here, or are you just visiting?"

"Visiting." Dana thought she saw something pass across John's face—disappointment maybe? She tried to get a better look at him, but didn't want to turn away from the sweet lady speaking to her now. *Was* he disappointed that she'd leave in a few weeks?

"Aw, that's too bad." Mary's eyes glanced from Dana to John. "Claremont's a great place to live. I was hoping that maybe you were staying for good."

Dana forced a smile but inside she knew that she was beginning to hope the same thing. She thought Claremont would be a great place to live, too. It seemed as if nothing could ever go wrong in the quaint country town.

Then she felt the first drop of rain.

Chapter Eight

April showers decided on an early arrival. Rain had poured through every one of John's four days off. Tonight he had to return to the steel plant, and he hadn't made any progress on getting the dude ranch up and running. Mandy Brantley hadn't been able to take any photos, because the trails were saturated and muddy. Casey hadn't made any headway on the website, because he needed the photos to determine the layout. Titus Jameson, the construction guy John had hired to grade the campsite area and build the supplies shack by the creek, couldn't get any of his equipment to the site because the fields resembled a swamp.

And on top of all that, six out of seven insurance companies John had contacted about insuring the dude ranch had turned him down flat. The only one left was the most expensive, and the price tag for the venture had climbed at a rapid pace already. Licenses and permits hadn't come cheap, and then there was the cost of construction, supplies and advertising. Thanks to his business marketing classes, he'd learned more and more each day about the astronomical cost of advertising his business. The dude ranch wasn't like the fish camp, relying on local word of mouth to keep the place filled. It wouldn't be a weekend getaway, but a family vacation. So John needed to advertise to people who would potentially schedule a week off work and school to visit the ranch.

How would Brooks International justify pouring so much money into an Alabama rancher's dream, especially when Dana had been down here to oversee the project for over a week, and nothing had happened? And for the past four days, because of the professors at Stockville trying to get in as much work as possible before next week's spring break, John hadn't spent nearly as much time with Dana as he would have liked. Two of his classes this semester had labs, and both of the labs habitually ran long and required extra work. Then today the rain, even heavier than it'd been every other day, kept him from getting to the farm and seeing Dana any quicker.

To make matters worse, he had to go back to work at the steel plant tonight. His four nights off had been pretty much wasted, as far as benefiting the ranch was concerned.

His windshield wipers beat a crazy rhythm as they attempted to slice through the endless sheet of water. Between the heavy rain and the windshield fogging over, he could barely see the road. The defroster, like most everything else on the old truck, hadn't worked in years, so he cranked down the window a little to clear up the fog on the glass. Unfortunately, that allowed a thin steady stream to spray John's side as he inched his way along the curvy wooded stretch leading to the farm.

Squinting to focus, he made out Eden Sanders's mailbox through the downpour. "One more mile." Finally, the entrance to the ranch came into view. Typically he'd forgo getting the mail in the driving rain, but his hope that the final insurance company would give the answer he wanted had him putting the truck in Park, slapping on his Stetson and climbing out. His boots plunged into a gigantic puddle, the dirt driveway now a minilake in the torrent. Rain streamed off his hat and, because the water came down at an angle, it also pelted his face. He reached the old silver mailbox, yanked it open and withdrew the small stack of letters and bills inside. Then he held them against his chest in an effort to keep the things dry as he sprinted back to the truck.

The envelopes were damp, and he flipped through junk mail and utility bills, tossing the discarded ones on the seat. The last envelope had the insurance company's logo, blurred from the rain, in the return address. *Dear God, give us what we need for the dude ranch.*

He pushed his finger along the edge of the envelope, opened it and withdrew the letter. Then he read a message that was almost word for word like the ones he'd received from all of the other companies.

No.

Dana didn't know when she'd had more fun. Eden, Georgiana and Abi alternated singing country songs and Christian contemporary music as they cooked. Dana joined in when she knew the words and helped them create the meal.

Dana Brooks cooking, preparing a casserole of all things. Ryan wouldn't believe it, but if her father were still around, he would. In one of their heartfelt conversations merely days before he died, he told her how he'd missed the simple joys of life while pursuing the almighty dollar. At his statement, she'd asked what he missed, and he'd answered, "I don't know, because I missed it, but don't you miss out, Dana." She had patted his hand and promised she wouldn't.

And here in the Cutter family kitchen, she found undeniable joy.

"Is this one ready for the marker?" Abi pointed to a broccoli, cheese and rice casserole that Eden had placed on the table to cool.

"I think so." Eden slid a green bean casserole in the oven, then covered the broccoli dish with a layer of heavy-duty foil.

"Can you hand me that marker, Miss Dana?"

"Sure." Dana put down the potato peeler and sweet potato, grabbed the Sharpie and placed it in the little girl's hand.

"Mama, can you spell this one for me? I know it's a *b* and an *r,* then what?" Abi wrote the two letters she knew on the top of the foil then waited, her tongue sticking out the side of her mouth as she concentrated.

Georgiana, cooking as well as any sighted person, stirred the brownie batter as she spelled out the remainder of *broccoli casserole* for her little girl. Abi's letters were perfect, for the most part, except for the second *r*, which looked a little more like a *p*.

"So how many do we have now?" Georgiana slid her palm along the counter, found the baking dish and poured the batter inside.

"Six casseroles and three main dishes." Eden rinsed her hands at the sink and then dried them off with a dish towel. "With everything the other ladies from church plan to make, we should have Mitch's freezer filled for quite some time." She peered out the window. "I just wish it wasn't raining so hard for when y'all deliver it."

"Maybe the rain will die down in a little while." Georgiana moved toward the sink with the mixing bowl, then paused and turned toward the table. "Abi, want to lick the bowl?"

"Yes, ma'am!"

Smiling, Georgiana stepped toward the table and Abi reached for the chocolate-coated bowl. "Rainy days are the best cooking days, aren't they?" Georgiana said to her little girl.

"Yes, ma'am." Abi licked the spoon and got her first taste of brownie batter.

For the past four days, the rain stopped occasionally, but even during those brief moments, dark clouds cloaked the sky. John had been particularly dismayed with the weather, since it prevented them from making any headway with the dude ranch. But Dana didn't mind the rain. When he went to the college each day, she stayed at the house with Georgiana, Eden and Abi. They'd had "girl time" in a way she'd never known, much better than hanging around her friends back home. There was no talk of upcoming notable events, no references to social status, nothing to put a damper on their optimism. Not even the weather.

Today they'd joined the church's effort to provide food for Mitch Gillespie while he adjusted to life without his wife. The meals didn't have to be overly large, since he only had himself and his three-year-old daughter to feed. His new baby girl would be on formula for a while and then baby food. Dana had been concerned about the young father ever since she learned his story at church Sunday, so helping to prepare the meals had been a pleasure. Even though she didn't know the man personally, she was glad that she could help. And silently she wondered if anyone had helped her father after her mother passed.

"I see some lights heading up the driveway. That'll be John." Eden left the kitchen and crossed the living area, peered out the front window in an effort to see.

"Or Landon. He should've been back from Doc Sheridan's by now," Georgiana said. "I hate that Sam got sick in the middle of this storm."

Dana had come to know all the animals around the farm over the past few days. *Sam,* short for *Samantha,* was the name of Landon's mare. Dana had learned that Landon received Sam as a gift from his father when he was eight, that the horse was probably in her last years and that Landon would do anything he could to keep her comfortable. Even if that meant going out in a storm for medicine.

"It's John." Eden continued peering at the drive. "And Landon is right behind him. They're both here."

"Thank goodness." Georgiana opened the oven door and called over her shoulder, "Is the top rack free?"

Dana looked at the casserole dishes on the middle rack. The top rack was empty. "Yes, it's free."

Georgiana slid the brownies in and then closed the door. "Abi, you want to fix a timer for the brownies? Twenty-five minutes."

Abi climbed off her chair and ran across the kitchen to pull yet another rectangular timer from the drawer. Several timers were sporadically spaced around the kitchen for the various dishes. "I picked a brown timer, so we'll know it's for the brownies."

"Great idea." Georgiana washed her hands and crossed the room toward the door as John, soaked through and through, hustled inside. "Landon?" she asked.

"No, it's me. Landon went out to the barn." John took off his Stetson, hung it on a hook by the door then pushed wet hair out of his eyes.

"Sam's sick," she told him. "I'm sure Landon wants to get her medicine to her as soon as he can."

Dana watched the exchange from the kitchen, the sweet potatoes she'd been peeling totally forgotten as her vision focused on John. His face was tense, brows dipped and mouth a flat line. No dimples to be seen. He looked up, locked eyes with hers, but the smile that she'd received almost every day when he came in was missing in action.

"You doing okay?" he asked Dana.

She nodded. "Yes, I'm fine." But she wasn't the one

who appeared *not* to be doing okay. Something had happened to him today. "How were your classes?"

"Okay." He didn't make any effort to walk toward the kitchen, as he had every other day upon arriving at the house, but moved toward the stairs. His clothes were drenched.

Dana had never seen a more beautiful man. Or a man who looked so disheartened. What had happened?

"I'm gonna go get some dry clothes." And with that, he started up the stairs, while Dana, confused, turned her attention back to peeling the sweet potatoes.

"Is Uncle John sad?" Abi asked, as if Dana had a way of knowing the answer.

"I don't know."

"When Daddy is sad, Mama makes him coffee." She propped her chin in her hand and watched the slivers of orange potato skin fall into the plastic trash can near Dana's knees. "Maybe you could make Uncle John some coffee to make him happy."

Eden grinned at her granddaughter. "That's a good idea, Abi. And it might take the chill of the rain off."

"Do you know how to make coffee yet?" The innocence of Abi's question made Dana laugh. She'd obviously paid attention to Dana's limitations in the kitchen. But thanks to Eden's and Georgiana's patience and instructions—not to mention detailed handwritten recipe cards—she was learning. And, thankfully, coffee was one of the few things she had mastered before she'd ever stepped foot in Claremont.

"Yes, I do know how to make coffee." She finished peeling the last sweet potato. "I'll make some—" she checked the recipe card "—then cut the sweet potatoes and put them on to boil."

Eden sat at the table. "Here, I'll cut them while you make the coffee. Georgiana, will you start the water for us?"

"Sure."

Dana didn't know when she'd felt more at ease around a group of people, or when she'd felt more like part of a family unit. It wasn't as though she hadn't grown up with a family; she'd had her father and Ryan, after all. But she couldn't recall a time where they had to work together to accomplish a goal. Even in business, they each had their own projects, their individual goals. On the other hand, the Cutter family joined hands to accomplish every task—whether major or trivial—around the house and around the farm. And they included Dana as though she belonged here.

"This is wonderful." She opened the lid on the coffee canister, and the scent of the ground coffee filled the air.

"Coffee does smell good, doesn't it?" Abi asked.

Dana nodded. "Yes, it does." But she hadn't been talking about the coffee. She was talking about her time with the Cutters. She finished preparing the coffeepot, turned it on then helped Eden with the dishes while she waited for the Cutter family member who'd made her feel the most wonderful of all, and the one who'd evidently had a hard day.

By the time she heard him start down the stairs, the coffee was done. She poured him a cup and met him in the living area. "Would you like some coffee?" She extended the mug.

John accepted the cup, his fingers brushing against her as he took it. "Thanks."

Dana lowered her voice. "Are—are you okay?"

He took a sip of the coffee, those amber eyes looking at her from over the rim, then he swallowed. "I will be, I guess." His head shook subtly, as though he wasn't sure what to say, what to do, and Dana wished there was some way she could help.

"What happened?" she whispered.

He took another sip of coffee. "Just not sure what God has planned for me right now. Maybe it isn't a dude ranch, after all."

The door bounded open and Landon came in, water pouring off his hat and his clothes dripping all over the towels Eden had put down after John's arrival. "I think Sam's doing better," he said. "Doc Sheridan said it's probably just a cold, but he gave me some meds to help."

"Horses get colds?" Dana's question was worth the laughs she got from the rest of the family, because it also produced a small smile from John.

He nodded. "Yep, just like their riders. And Sam is typically too interested in what's happening in the field to come in out of the rain."

"She just likes knowing what's going on." Abi crossed the room and started to hug Landon, but then planted her feet on the hardwood floor. "Whoa, you're all wet. I'll hug you after you change your clothes."

Landon's smile and the glint of mischievousness in his eyes gave Abi a slight warning, and she turned to run, but his arm reached out and snagged her. He pulled her to his wet chest and kissed her cheeks while she giggled.

"You're—you're getting me all wet!" She squealed and laughed.

"Landon—" Georgiana barely contained her own smile "—now she'll have to change her clothes, too."

Georgiana couldn't see Landon to know what was coming, but everyone else did, and she must have suspected that he'd released Abi and turned his focus on his wife.

"Oh, Landon, don't you dare." She turned and started toward the kitchen, but he caught her in two strides, pulled her close and rubbed his face against her neck while she—and everyone else—laughed.

Eventually, they all went upstairs to change, since Georgiana and Abi were nearly as wet as Landon, and Eden, John and Dana moved to the kitchen to get the table ready for dinner.

"That was precious," Eden said. "It does me good to see them all so happy."

John poured himself another cup of coffee. "I'm glad, too."

Dana had seen him laughing at his brother's display, but now he'd sobered again, and she suspected that he could also use a bit of happiness. But he'd seemed happy over the past week, even if a little disappointed in the weather. Tonight, however, he didn't. And she had no idea what he'd meant about God not having it in His plan for John to run the dude ranch.

One of her strengths at Brooks International had been identifying strategies and fixing problems with investments. By the time they finished dinner, she had no doubt that John's mood had something to do with a problem with his business. And after Eden left for her home, and Georgiana, Landon and Abi went to deliver the casseroles to Mitch, she'd decided that it was time to put her talents to work here and, one way or another, fix John's problem, too.

He poured another cup of coffee, glanced at Dana. "You want a cup?"

"Sure."

"What do you take in it?" He filled his mug, took another from the cabinet and filled it, as well.

"Just black."

He nodded. "Georgiana puts so much milk in hers, it's barely brown. And Abi, well, we make her coffee milk just so she'll feel big."

"That's precious." Dana took the mug, sipped the hot liquid. "That's three cups for you, isn't it? Aren't you a little worried that you won't sleep?"

"Figured I'd just stay up until it was time to go to the plant. I'll sleep a couple of hours in the morning before my first class."

"That's not enough rest, is it?"

"I'll try to grab a few hours before tomorrow night's shift, too." He leaned against the counter, continued drinking the coffee and sighed audibly. Even his tone was different than it'd been all week, and Dana hated hearing the loss of hope.

"It sounds like the rain has stopped. Would you like to go sit on the porch?" She knew he liked sitting outside at night and viewing the fields. They'd ended each day that way since she'd arrived at the farm.

He nodded. "I'll grab a couple of towels in case the rockers are wet." He walked from the kitchen to the adjoining laundry room, then returned carrying two thick towels. Apparently, he finished his coffee while walking, because he placed the empty mug in the sink.

Not wanting too much caffeine this late, Dana took another sip of hers, put her cup beside his in the sink and then followed him out to the rockers on the porch.

A rain-scented breeze blew across the fields, and Dana inhaled the gentle fragrance as she rocked. She didn't want to barrel right into asking him why he'd lost his enthusiasm for the dude ranch, so she selected a nice, neutral topic. The weather—or, rather, the fact that it would change soon. "The meteorologist said the rain should move out tonight."

His rocker creaked as he moved back and forth. "I heard that on the radio when I was driving home."

Dana watched a group of cows slowly move higher on a hill, she assumed to get out of the saturated low spots. She saw the gray clouds shift and spotted a brief hint of the moon attempting to peek through the thick barricade. The ranch always appealed to Dana, but after the storm, its beauty was captivating. Yet the rancher beside her stared straight ahead, definitely not paying attention to his surroundings tonight.

She waited as long as she could, then asked, "What happened? Why don't you think it's God's plan for you to start a dude ranch?" It still felt a little odd discussing God as though she knew Him, but bit by bit through the week, she'd begun to feel that she did, or at least that she was getting closer to knowing Him the way she wanted to.

Even in the dimness of the porch, she saw John's jaw tighten. He slowly rocked back and forth a couple of times, then finally answered, "I can't have a dude ranch if I can't get the place insured."

A small red flag went off amid her plans for the ranch. Insurance. She'd known he'd need insurance for guests at the ranch, but she hadn't thought he'd have any problem getting approved. "You're having trouble getting insurance?"

"I only found seven companies that would even consider insuring a dude ranch from someone with no experience."

Before he could continue, Dana interjected. "You have experience. This ranch has been in your family since before you were born, right? What more do they want?"

"Experience in business—specifically a dude ranch business. And the fish camp doesn't count, since it is basically only a site rental. The dude ranch will have activities—lots of activities—where guests could presumably get injured. Therefore, I need more insurance. And I need a history with running dude ranches."

Dana understood the companies' point, but that didn't make her any happier about it. "We'll find insurance."

"I'm telling you, I requested a quote from every place I could find that insures places like this. You'd have thought from their letters that they all got together on their reasoning for turning me down." He shrugged. "The ranch is a risk—too big of a risk for them to take." A couple of beats passed, then he pushed up from the rocker and stood. "You should think about that, Dana. This is probably too big a risk for you to take, too. And I'm not into wasting other people's money." He cleared his throat. "No matter how much money they have."

"But I'm sure we can find some insurance for the ranch."

He'd already moved to the steps. "We may need to cut our losses. On top of the insurance problem, I hadn't thought about the potential for rain. All of our fishing camp guests canceled for this weekend, thinking the place would be too swampy, and if the sun doesn't come out in full force tomorrow and Saturday, it will be. When it rains like that, the dude ranch won't be any good to tourists, either."

"You could offer rain checks to people booked on the rainy days."

He lifted a shoulder. "Maybe. But if I can't insure them, we won't have any guests here, anyway." His boots slapped against the wet ground as he left the porch and started toward his truck. He hadn't been able to ride Red to his cabin since Sunday, and he had to drive the truck and leave it parked in the driveway near his place each night. Dana figured the fact that he couldn't end his day riding his horse only added to his gloomy disposition. "I'll see you tomorrow. And if you do decide this isn't what you want to invest in and you want to head back to Chicago, I'll understand."

She watched him walk away, her throat thick with

emotion at seeing the strong cowboy at his breaking point. He backed up the truck, lifted a hand and drove away.

Then Dana fished her cell phone from her pocket and wasted no time dialing.

Ryan answered on the second ring. "Meanwhile, back at the ranch…"

"Not funny. Listen, I need some help…"

Chapter Nine

"Are you done yet?" Abi kept her head turned away, her freckled face scrunched in dismay while John put the worm on her hook.

Dana still hadn't got used to watching the process, either, so she kept her eyes on Abi while John quickly finished the task and released the bait toward the water.

"All done and ready to go, but try to wait a little longer before catching a fish this time. I can't keep my line in the water when I have to keep baiting yours." He tapped Abi's shoulder. "You really shouldn't be such a good fishing lady already. I'm just sayin'."

"I can't help it—I'm good." Abi nodded her head and sent strawberry-colored pigtails bouncing in the process. Her red-and-white cork hit the top of the water, and she coaxed, "Come on, little fishy, bite. I'm gonna catch more than Uncle John, 'cause he's gotta keep baiting my hook."

Dana hid her grin behind her hand, and John winked at her from his spot on the other side of his niece.

Thankfully, his dour mood over the insurance problem had disappeared since he'd told Dana about his dilemma two nights ago. But since then, he'd completely stopped talking about the dude ranch. And he'd mentioned a couple of times that Dana should enjoy a few things around the farm before she headed back to Chicago, as though he'd already dismissed the concept of the dude ranch and presumed she couldn't wait to head home.

Wrong on both counts. The dude ranch *would* be insured and ready to go; he'd find that out soon. And Dana had no desire to go home. None at all. In fact, she rather dreaded it. She didn't want to leave the ranch, didn't want to leave the quaintness of Claremont and sure didn't want to leave the handsome, compassionate cowboy currently pointing a warning finger at his niece as she brought yet another fish out of the water and held it in front of his face.

"What did I tell you?" he asked.

Abi laughed so hard she snorted.

John deftly removed the bream from the hook and tossed it back in the water. Then he tweaked Abi's pigtail. "You weren't supposed to catch any more, not that quick, anyway."

"And I told you—" her small shoulders shook with her giggle "—I can't help it if I'm good."

Since the campsites for the ranch were still too wet to set up tents, Abi had settled for a fishing trip before her Daddy picked her up for spring break. But she made sure John and Dana knew she expected to go camping when she got back.

"There, you're ready to go again." John released the

hooked worm toward the water, where it fell in, and then the cork...promptly headed south.

"Hah! That's the fastest catch yet!" Abi yanked up the line and, sure enough, another fat bream hung from the hook.

"I'm telling you, that's the same fish." John removed the hook then held the shiny bream toward Abi.

The little girl shook her head with gusto. "Nope, the last one didn't have that kind of eyes."

John looked skeptical. "You think you can see a difference in their eyes?"

"Yep. That one has sad eyes." She leaned forward, tilted her head and got a good look. "Sad, aren't you?" Then she glanced up at John. "The other one had sweet eyes."

"If you ask me, they're probably all sad because you took them out of the water and away from their home."

Abi moved her face even closer to the fish. "And that's why we put you back in."

He grinned. "Yes, that's why. So, do you want to put her back in this time?"

Abi studied the bream again. "How do you know it's a girl?"

"Just guessing."

"I think it's a boy." She nodded her head with the statement, as though already determining the fact.

"All right. So do you want to put *him* back in?"

Abi hadn't touched a fish yet, but Dana could tell curiosity was getting the better of her. "If you help me, I will."

"Okay. You can hold him two ways. The first is you

put your thumb in his mouth and pinch a little, like this." John demonstrated holding up the fish.

Abi's hazel eyes grew big. "What's the other way?"

He grinned. "The other way is to cup your hands around him like this, and don't worry, his gills won't hurt you."

Abi's hands drew into little fists. "But Mama said some gills do hurt you. She told me to be careful. She said it today, when I told her we were going fishing."

John nodded. "Catfish gills. That's what she's talking about. This is just a little bream."

"He looks like a big bream to me."

John checked his grin. "He's big for a bream, but he's much smaller than those big ol' catfish that live on the bottom of the pond. And his gills won't hurt you, I promise." He eased the fish into Abi's waiting palms. "See?"

"Hey, he doesn't feel slimy at all," Abi said in surprise. "Just kind of cold. And wet." She looked at Dana. "You want to feel him?"

Dana did her best not to make a face. "I think I'll save that for another day."

John laughed. "It isn't bad, is it, Abi?"

"Nope, not bad." She peered into the fish's eyes again. "Hey there, fish. I'm the one who caught you, but I'm gonna let you go back to swim again now, okay?" She lifted her brows as though waiting for the bream to answer, then smiled, leaned toward the edge and gently released the fish into the water.

The low rumble of an engine and crunching gravel alerted them that a vehicle had started up the driveway.

Dana looked up to see a black Mercedes slowing near the fence, the tinted window easing down and a man's face coming into view. He was the city version of attractive, and Dana got the strangest sense of pleasure that she only noticed him as that, a good-looking city guy. She turned toward the cowboy on the other side of the patchwork quilt, the rancher who'd spent the past hour helping his niece fish, and she inwardly saluted the differences between this man and the one in the car.

The city boy was fake, money-made, living-an-easy-life attractive. But the tall, muscled, hardworking cowboy lounging on the quilt—now *that* was Dana's idea of handsome.

She noticed John made no effort to get up and go greet the other guy. In fact, his face turned into a semi-snarl.

"Abi, what are you doing out there getting all dirty before we go on our trip? You knew I was coming this afternoon, didn't you? I told you this morning to be ready when I got here."

"I am ready. I just wanted to go fishing for a little bit until you got here, Daddy."

"I haven't got a lot of time to wait for you to get cleaned up before we leave," he said, his mouth tense, but then he appeared to force a smile. "And we've got several fun stops to make along the way back to Tampa."

"Really?" Abi quickly handed her pole to her uncle. "Don't worry, Daddy. I'm not that dirty. I don't even smell like fish yet." She took a whiff of her hand to make sure then shrugged. "Well, not too bad. I'll wash my hands." Abi gave John a quick hug. "I've got to go. Love you!"

"I love you, sweetie."

Then she hugged Dana. "Bye, Miss Dana. Love you, too!"

Dana's heart clenched so tight it hurt. She'd never had a child tell her that she loved her, and the tender words sent a rush of warmth through her soul. She blinked back tears. "I love you, too, Abi," she whispered, accepting the precious hug and realizing the words were so very, very true.

She did love this little girl. And, glancing at John, she wondered...*am I falling in love with you, too?*

Abi's father finally got out of his car, opened the gate and hesitantly stepped into the pasture as though worried he might get something on his shoes. He dressed like Ryan—tailored shirt, dress slacks, expensive shoes. But he did accept his daughter's running hug with open arms, even if his face cringed a bit when he inhaled.

"We may have to wait for you to take a bath first," he said.

"Is that okay?" Abi's lower lip ran out a tad. "I didn't mean to smell fishy."

"It's fine. I'll just move our dinner reservations. It isn't a problem." Though his tone said it was.

Abi didn't seem to notice. "Great! You want to come say hey to Uncle John and meet Miss Dana? She's from Chicago." Abi had finally converted the "windy town" to Chicago after hearing her parents and John reference the city several times throughout the past week. Funny thing, though. Dana missed being known as the girl from the windy town rather than the lady from the prominent city.

"Hello, Pete." John didn't stand to meet the guy, so Dana kept her place on the quilt, too.

"Cutter. I see you're overly busy today. Georgiana had said your fish camp was doing well. Only one customer this weekend?" He tilted his head toward Dana.

"Actually—" John glared, the soft amber in his eyes converting to an intense gold "—we don't have any paid guests this weekend, due to all the rain."

"So I guess it isn't doing as well as my ex implied." He nodded. "Figures."

"The camp is doing fine." John's words were pushed through gritted teeth, and his look said he dared the guy to argue the point.

Pete apparently took the hint and turned his attention to Dana. "So you aren't here for the fish camp?"

"No, I'm here for the dude ranch." She saw John's shoulders tense with her statement, but this man had irritated her, too, and she wanted to put him in his place.

"Dude ranch? What dude ranch is that?" Pete's sinister smile made her skin crawl.

"I'm investing in John's newest project, converting their farm into a dude ranch. It's going to be amazing. Guests will participate in trail rides, horseback riding, camping, a true outdoor vacation. Many people never have the opportunity to experience that anymore, but they will here, at the Cutter Dude Ranch, and they'll learn the history of the dude ranch from John."

"A dude ranch, in Alabama? You don't say?"

Abi bobbed her head. "Yep, and I'm going to help

the kids learn about riding horses, so I've been taking lots and lots of extra lessons from Grandma. And Uncle John and Miss Dana are going to let me go camping with them when we don't get so much rain and all, and we're going to cook marshmallows and hot dogs and sing songs and stuff. It's going to be great!"

John didn't release his smile, but the impression of both dimples dipped in and Dana sensed his pride at Abi's excitement. Even though he didn't think the dude ranch was going to make it, he was still proud of the effort.

Dana couldn't wait until he checked today's mail.

"So you're from Chicago? And you're investing in a dude ranch in Alabama?" Pete cleared his throat. "I'm sure John probably told you, but I'm a partner in a very successful investment firm in Tampa. And there's no way we would touch anything as risky and uncertain as a dude ranch in Alabama." He grinned, but it wasn't a friendly smile. "Guess they must do things different up there in Chicago." His head shook subtly, his disbelief evident, as he looked from John to Dana. "Good luck to you and your little investment, Miss Dana."

"You can call her Miss Brooks." John's voice was nearly a growl, his anger contained, but barely.

Pete had already turned to walk away, but he shifted on his heel, took another look at Dana. And then she saw it when the pieces clicked into place. "Miss *Brooks?* Dana Brooks?" His cheeks swiftly reddened. "From Brooks International?"

"You've heard of the company?" John's tone was

mocking, but Dana didn't blame him. This guy had ticked her off, too.

"Yes, Brooks International," she said. "We're very excited about the dude ranch potential in northern Alabama and thrilled to have people as hardworking, trustworthy and experienced as the Cutter family who can pull it off." She used the same tone she used in the boardroom when describing a potential investment, one that she was certain would succeed. "We're anticipating a huge profit margin with this venture, so I came down personally to oversee the start-up." She lifted a shoulder. "But that's just the way we do things in Chicago."

John's laugh nearly escaped, but he quickly made it seem as if he were merely clearing his throat.

Pete's jaw dropped open, then he visibly worked to snap it closed. Apparently, he'd run out of snobbish things to say.

"You ready for me to go wash the fish off, Daddy? I'm excited about our week together, aren't you?" Abi tugged at Pete's hand, and the guy finally relented.

"Yes, let's go." His words were directed to his daughter, but the confusion in his tone was clearly directed at Dana.

Dana smiled. "Nice to meet you." Then she frowned; that was an absolute lie. She'd have to work on her response in the future, now that she had decided to get her life on track. No more lies for the sake of the business. No more associating with people like Pete. She wanted to surround herself with honesty, with faith and, she now realized, with love.

Pete and Abi got in his car, and Abi waved as they

continued down the driveway toward the main house. Dana and John waved back. And Pete looked straight ahead, refusing to glance back at the couple by the pond.

The car moved out of sight, then Dana heard John's low rumble of a chuckle and turned to see him drop his back to the quilt and release the laughter with full force. "You were priceless," he said, beaming. "I'd almost think you knew him as long as I have. You sure pushed his buttons."

She laughed. "I do know him. He's every guy I have to deal with in Chicago. All full of themselves and ready to brag about even the smallest accomplishment. It really gets annoying, doesn't it?"

"It sure does." He turned to his side and looked at her. "Every guy in the city is like that?"

"I suppose every guy isn't, but every guy I deal with is." She thought about the people she dealt with on a regular basis, all of them after the biggest profit and most of them forming friendships and networks based on what they could get out of each relationship. "When I'm in Chicago, I think I'm at a disadvantage when it comes to learning what people are really like. And probably at a disadvantage when it comes to meeting people who are willing to be themselves around me."

"What do you mean?"

"Most of my relationships are formed in and around Brooks International, so everyone knows me because of the company. And they figure that's enough, I suppose. So they don't take the time to get to know me as a person." She thought about the superficial relationships that filled her life, and sighed. "When people meet me there and hear my name, they usually react the same way Pete did a moment ago. And it's all fake. Makes it difficult to form true friendships, you know?"

His look was warm and tender, and Dana had no doubt he understood. "You really like it here, don't you?"

She didn't hesitate. "I love it here."

"Yeah, I can tell you do." He rolled onto his back, laced his fingers and put them under his head as he gazed at the blue sky overhead. "I'm sure that threw Pete for a loop, seeing that someone like you could be happy here. Most folks around here who go and get a taste of the big city leave and don't come back. Guess they see it as greener pastures, so to speak."

Dana knew he was talking about the girl who'd broken his heart. Georgiana had mentioned MaciJo a couple of times during the week, and Maribeth had also said something about her breaking John's heart. Dana couldn't stand the thought of anyone hurting him, and she didn't want him to doubt how much she wanted to be here, on the ranch, and, more importantly, with him. "Obviously they weren't paying attention to what they had right here. Because if I'd been raised in a place as beautiful as this, with people as wonderful as the people in Claremont, I'd never have wanted to leave."

His gaze moved from the sky back to Dana. "That's the way I feel, exactly. I've got to admit that it's surprising that you feel the same way, but it's a nice surprise."

"To be honest, it surprised me how much I like it here, but you really have to experience it to understand how amazing it is—the beauty of the fields, the mountains, the town and the people. I couldn't get over people greeting me and chatting with me when we went to the square. The friendliness is almost, well, shocking when you come from the city."

"I don't expect I'd handle dealing with that every day very well, people passing by each other and not saying a word. That just isn't the way we do things down here." His mouth crooked up on one side. "I probably wouldn't handle dealing with people like Pete every day very well, either, but I have to admit, you handled him well."

Dana liked the way he grinned at her, as though he was proud of the fact that she'd put Pete in his place. "Did you see how red his cheeks got? Does he always do that?"

Her question caused another rolling laugh. "I did see, and yeah, I've seen his cheeks get red when he's nervous. He was the star quarterback on our football team in high school. But any time he got sacked, those cheeks went to flaming. Oh, and it was always his offensive line's fault when something happened to him. The great Pete Watson could do no wrong."

"I'm sure that same philosophy followed him into business. Probably spends the majority of his time shifting the blame for his own bad investments." She knew the type, hated the type.

"I'm sure he does." He pushed up from the quilt, and his smile faded a little. "I appreciate your telling him about the investment and all, but I realize there's no way to pull this thing off without insurance."

A couple of horses came into view in the distance, their pelts glistening in the afternoon sun as they galloped across the field. John looked at the pair, then cleared his throat. "Listen, I know that the dude ranch isn't going to happen, and that there really isn't any reason for you to stay in Alabama. There's no way Brooks International will invest in a place that can't get insurance." He swallowed then turned to look directly at Dana, and she saw the sadness in those beautiful amber eyes.

"You may still get insurance," she said, and was about to tell him more, but he shook his head.

"I haven't even requested quotes anywhere else. There's no one left to ask. But I want you to know how much I've enjoyed having you here and how amazing it is to see you appreciate the ranch, the town, everything. I mean, if you'd like to stay a little longer and see a few more of the sights, I'd like to show you around. Granted, I still have two more nights of third shift at the plant, but then I'll have four nights off and spring break from college. I was going to ask if you would stay till the end of next week and let me show you around."

"I'd like that, very much," she said, picturing the tour of the town from John's perspective and all of the time together. She loved being alone with him, times like right now, sitting by a pond, with the fields surrounding them, livestock grazing nearby and the beauty of the mountains in the distance. No, she didn't plan to leave at the end of next week. She planned on their being busier than ever getting the dude ranch running, but she also wanted the experience John described, having him show her around. Just the two of them.

"All the rain has prevented us from doing things I

think you'd enjoy, things I'd like for you to see. One of the trails, the one that leads by our old tree house, goes all the way to the town square. If the dude ranch would have worked, I'd planned to let that be one day's main activity, a trail ride or a hike to the square. I thought I could meet with the local merchants and artists there and ask them to offer some type of frontier specials to the dude ranch guests." He shrugged. "Not sure if that'd have been as big a hit as I anticipated, but I thought it was a decent idea. Plus, it could've potentially generated some business for the shop owners."

"That's an amazing idea," Dana said, happy to hear him describing his plans again, even if he thought of them only as a missed opportunity. "And I think you should definitely do that one day for the main activity. Maybe you could even name that trail something that would go along with the theme of heading into the town." She thought about potential trail names. "What could you call it?"

"I'd thought about the Supplies and Vittles Run," he said, grinning. "You know, like when the early settlers came across a town and would shop for supplies and food. Maybe that's a little too quirky."

"No, it's not. It's adorable."

"Adorable. Yep, that's what I was going for. That's mighty appealing to a man's ego to know that his name for a rustic trail ride is 'adorable.' Goes right up there with 'precious,' don't ya think?"

She laughed. "*Awesome?* It's awesome? Or what about *rugged.* How's that for a manly word?"

"Better than adorable."

"Okay, *rugged* it is. And you should definitely run with that idea for the ranch."

"If there was going to be a ranch."

"I wanted to talk to you about that. And I meant to tell you that you *haven't* heard from all the insurance companies yet."

"Yeah, I did. I only found seven that would even consider providing insurance for this type of place, and I have the seven rejection letters to prove that each and every one of them turned me down flat."

"But you haven't heard from the insurance companies *I* contacted. I requested quotes from a few places affiliated with Brooks International."

His brows lifted, eyes locked with hers. "You contacted companies? Why didn't you say anything?"

"I thought yours would come through. Mine was just a backup, in case we didn't get the answer we wanted from the ones you contacted." She didn't add that she'd never contacted any until after their conversation two nights ago. Or that she'd had to ask Ryan to help find a company willing to take the risk of insuring the ranch. And she also didn't mention that they could probably buy an entire farm for what she'd had to spend on the high-risk coverage.

She wouldn't tell John any of that, because all she wanted him to know was that he would have insurance, and he would have the dude ranch of his dreams. Dana would make certain of it.

"And have you heard from any of yours?" he asked.

"Not yet." But she knew they would hear today. The agent verified that the acceptance letter would be sent via overnight delivery when Dana called him yesterday afternoon and told him he could expect more business from Brooks International in the future once John Cutter's application was approved.

John's look of hope dropped a little. "Listen, I appreciate your trying to help, but I wouldn't expect a different answer. As I told you before, all those rejection letters looked like they were written by the same person. They all have the same reasons for denying our coverage, and even if I'm not happy about it, their reasons do make sense." He gave her a small grin. "I probably wouldn't insure me, either."

"We won't know until we hear from them." She glanced toward the driveway. "Have you checked today's mail?"

"Didn't think I had a reason to."

"Well, now you do." She pushed up from the quilt to stand, then turned and reached out her hand. "Come on, let's go check. You might get the news you've been waiting for. You never know."

He ignored her statement about the potential for good news and instead concentrated on her outstretched hand. "You really think you can pull me up?"

"Abi said these boots give your feet a better grip on the ground. I might as well see." She'd worn the pink mud boots that she'd bought from Maribeth because, in spite of the fact that the rain had stopped, the ground was still extremely mushy in spots.

"It isn't your feet getting a better grip that I'm worried about. It's the fact that I can't quite see all a hundred and ten pounds of you lifting all nearly two hundred pounds of me, and I don't want you to hurt yourself trying."

"You underestimate me, *and* my weight," she said, wiggling her fingers, "but I'm not going to give you any additional info about that. Come on, let me try. I might just surprise you."

"I'm guessing lots of people underestimate you, Ms. Brooks," he said with a grin, and he put his hand in hers.

She felt the calluses of his palm, watched the way the tan fingers twined between her lighter ones and felt a frisson of delight at the mere touch of his skin to hers. If he thought she'd go back to Chicago anytime in the near future, he thought wrong. She was nowhere near ready to leave the ranch, and definitely nowhere near ready to leave John. Whatever was going on between them was just getting started and was more exciting than anything she'd experienced in a very long time, and she couldn't wait to see where it led.

Planting her feet, she pulled on his hand, and he helped her, of course, by easing up from the ground. But even so, the shift in his weight and the fact that she pulled caused his momentum to move forward, and the next thing Dana knew she'd basically yanked herself into his chest.

She inhaled, smelled the woodsy scent that had captivated her ever since she arrived on the farm. Then she heard the soft thunder of his heart against her ear. And she didn't make any effort to move.

He cleared his throat. "Guess I did underestimate you. You pulled me up."

She took a small, very small, step back. "I believe you helped."

"Maybe a little, but that was a good effort."

"Thanks."

"So, you have some sort of women's intuition that we'll find good news in the mail today?"

"Something like that."

"Okay, but I'm warning you. I haven't gotten any good news out of that box this week."

"Then I'd say you're due, don't you think?"

"You always see the cup as half full, don't you?" he asked, as they walked across the field.

"That's funny, I thought that about you."

"Until this week."

"The week isn't over yet." She grinned, looking forward to the moment he found that letter in the mail.

He opened the gate and let her pass through. "No, it isn't. Who knows, maybe you're right and some insurance company sent a letter giving us every bit of coverage we need to start a dude ranch in Alabama."

His tone leaned toward the sarcastic, but Dana merely nodded. "Maybe so."

He shook his head at the crazy idea, then moved to the silver mailbox and opened it.

Dana's heart raced, especially when she saw the thin cardboard that signaled an overnight letter. "What's that?"

He left the other pieces of mail in the box, his attention focused on the red, white and blue mailer with the eagle stamped across the side. "I've never heard of this insurance company." He tapped the return address.

"That's because it's one that I submitted to," she said excitedly. "So, open it. See what it says."

He closed his eyes, kept them that way for a moment, and Dana had no doubt that he was praying. So she said a silent prayer, too.

God, let all of this work out. Please don't let him find out how I got the insurance. Let everything go smoothly from now on, and let the dude ranch be a huge success. And, if it be Your will, let him start feeling toward me what I'm feeling toward him. She opened her eyes to find John holding a paper in his hand and smiling. "What does it say?"

"It says—" he grabbed her in a hug and let out an excited yell that caused Dana to jump, then he pulled back enough for her to see the happiness in his eyes, the joy in his smile "—it says…that we are going to have a dude ranch."

Chapter Ten

John couldn't believe how quickly things turned around after he received the letter stating that he had the insurance coverage. Now they really had to get a move on in order to get everything done before Dana took their results back to the Brooks International board. Granted, the megacompany had already decided to invest, but he wanted them to be happy with their choice. More than that, he knew how important it was to Dana, and the only way to get the board behind her for future investments was to make sure this one turned out to be a wise move on her part.

So John was thrilled that he had a week off from college for spring break, giving him more time to work on the ranch...and more time to spend with Dana. He didn't miss the fact that she'd be leaving in merely twenty days. He only had twenty more days with the woman who was on his mind 24/7, whether they were together, working on the ranch, or apart. He'd tried to control the attraction, the admiration and the affection that he felt toward the city girl, but day by day, he felt himself falling hard.

After the pain of MaciJo leaving him high and dry, he hadn't wanted to get hurt again. Therefore, he'd tried to barricade his heart, offer some sort of protection against the inevitable moment when Dana would leave his ranch and go back to the snazzy city guys and upscale lifestyle that he'd never be able to afford—and a lifestyle that he would never want, truth be told. But his big ol' country heart wouldn't listen.

"Hey, are you even listening to me?" She shoved her shoulder against his arm as they hiked the trail that led to the town square. Then she stopped walking and stood with her hands on her hips. Incredible how she could still look classily pretty in a cowboy hat, Western shirt, jeans and pink boots. The pink boots, naturally, were what set her apart from every other cowgirl he knew in Claremont. And she apparently loved the cute accessory. She wore them everywhere. But right now, one of those boots tapped against the ground as she attempted to show mock irritation and she lifted a suspicious blond brow in his direction. "You haven't heard anything I've said, have you? Probably too busy planning more things for the dude ranch instead of listening to me ramble, huh?"

He grinned. *Huh* had entered her vocabulary over the past few days. He was pretty certain she'd never used the term at any of her business settings in Chicago. But she used it well now, and looked adorable doing it. "Honestly, no. I had my mind on other things." Not plans for the ranch, but plans for getting up the nerve to tell her what he was feeling for her. If only she wasn't leaving in three weeks—and potentially leaving his heart in tatters at the same time—it'd sure make things a whole lot easier.

"Well, I thought it was a good idea, but if it didn't even hold your attention, maybe not." She nudged back the cowboy hat she'd borrowed from Georgiana so she could look at him better, and John took advantage of the moment to look at her, too.

Her blue eyes reminded him of the photos he'd seen online of Caribbean waters. Her pretty face outdid any model's in a magazine, her straight white-blond hair fell past her shoulders and tempted him to reach out and touch it, to feel the soft silk against his fingers.

"John?"

He laughed. One way or another, he had to get a grip on this attraction. "Yeah?"

She tilted her head as though trying to determine what he'd been thinking.

"Come on, we need to keep walking if we want to have a little time at the square before we have to start back. It doesn't get dark until seven, but it's already after four and we still have another half-hour hike before we get there. Then you'll want to shop, I assume."

She pointed out the obvious. "I can't shop too much, because we'll have to carry everything back."

"I hadn't thought of that. We'll need to make sure our guests have a way to get their things back." They'd been busy the past two days giving direction to Titus Jameson about how they wanted the campsites laid out, where they needed the supply shack by the creek and how they wanted the trails cleared out enough for multiple riders. This afternoon they'd decided to hike the trail to the square and take note of how long it took to walk it, as well as what types of activities could be incorporated into this particular trail for guests.

"Your guests wouldn't have to tote everything back at all if you had the shop owners keep a tab for them during the week and then deliver the items to the ranch at the end of their stay."

He liked watching her mind at work. "That's a great idea."

"Yeah, my other idea was pretty good, too—" she wagged her finger at him "—but you weren't listening."

"Try me again. I'm all ears." A big log lay across the path, and he took her hand to help her over it. "We'll need to get Titus and his guys to move this for sure."

"Definitely." She stepped up and over the log.

John could have released her hand, but he didn't. And her attention moved to where their fingers were joined, her eyes easing up to reach his.

"Okay if I hold your hand?" He sounded like a nervous teenager.

She slid each of her fingers between each of his, her small palm easily fitting within his larger one. "Yes."

They started walking again, and John expected her to tell him about the idea he'd missed when he'd been daydreaming. But she didn't speak, and he wondered if she was feeling the same undeniable attraction. From the flush on her cheeks, he guessed that this thing wasn't at all one-sided.

"So, are you going to tell me that idea, or are you waiting for me to beg or something?"

Her nervous laugh echoed through the trees. "Oh, yeah, right." She cleared her throat. "Okay, what I was thinking is that you could talk to the merchants on the town square about having some kind of scavenger hunt for your guests, where they are supposed to find items specific to each of the stores. We could even talk to the merchants today when we get to the square so they can start considering the idea."

"A scavenger hunt?" He could see guests enjoying the activity, but wasn't sure whether the shop owners would want people scouring through their stores each week for items, especially if the process didn't benefit their businesses.

"Hang on. I've got it figured out. See, the shopowners would need to have the products on hand, small trinkets that would compliment the theme of the store. It wouldn't be a random item, but something that'd been preplanned by you and the merchants. Maybe you could charge a scavenger hunt fee as part of your activities fees. Guests who wanted to participate in the scavenger hunt would pay that fee, and you could give that money to the store owners to cover the cost of the items."

"And the scavenger item would advertise the store and potentially convince our guests to make a few purchases there, as well." John followed her reasoning, and liked it.

"Yes, and to get everything on their list, they'd have to visit each store, which also provides the shop owners with a chance to show off their merchandise and maybe even share a little about the town at the same time. You could have a few Claremont history questions as part of the hunt. You know, they'd have to get answers to ten questions about Claremont, and they'd get those answers from some of the store owners." She shrugged. "Something like that."

John thought about all the people he knew at the town square and how they were always interested in a way to boost business in the town's sole shopping area. "I can just imagine Mr. Crowe at the barbershop sitting our guests down in one of his old black leather barber chairs and telling them all about the town. He's in his late eighties now and loves to chat about the good ol' days."

"We'll put him on the list for answering a history question. Maybe you can even offer bonus points to guests who get a haircut from Mr. Crowe while they're at the square."

He laughed. "That'd make his day." John loved the older man who'd cut his hair his entire life, as well as his father's and his grandfather's. And Mr. Crowe loved company. No doubt all the guests from the ranch would benefit from getting to meet the sweet elderly man, but Mr. Crowe would benefit, too, because he'd have that many more people to visit with each day. "I really like that idea, incorporating the merchants in the scavenger hunt, and especially the haircut bonus. I can't wait to tell Mr. Crowe."

"See, I told you it was a good idea." She nodded her head and smiled triumphantly.

"All right now, you're quickly slipping from overly cute to overly confident," he warned.

"Overly cute? *That's* how you see me?" She tilted her nose in the air and grinned. "I could get used to that."

"As I said, you *were* there, but you've moved right on into overly confident." And charming. And heart-stoppingly pretty.

She punched his arm, and John laughed.

"Okay, okay, you're cute."

That only made her punch him harder.

"Overly cute," she reminded, "*that's* what you said."

"That *is* what I said."

"For the record, you aren't too shabby yourself, if I'm being completely—" Her phone beeped loudly, and she stopped midsentence. "Oh, hey, I must have caught a signal." She fished her cell out of her pocket and read the text. "Shockingly, it isn't from Ryan."

"Maybe he gave up on trying to reach you out here in the sticks." John smirked. The few times Ryan had gotten through to Dana in John's presence, the guy's irritation with the limitations of living on the ranch were undeniable, even if John only heard Dana's side of the conversation.

"Maybe he did. But this text is from Mandy Brantley." She scanned the message. "She has the photos ready for your review and sent a link to see them on her site."

Mandy had visited the ranch after church on Sunday and had taken an abundance of photos of the trails, the waterfall and the creek. She'd told John and Dana that she probably wouldn't have the pictures ready until later in the week, but she must have sensed their urgency, because today was only Tuesday, and she was done. "That's great. Can you bring them up on your phone?"

"I'm trying." She tapped the screen. "The signal is getting weak again."

"I guess we can wait till we get to the square to take a look. As soon as we see them, though, I want to forward them to Casey. He's itching to put them on the site. He went ahead and designed the basic layout, navigation and all, but he still needs the photos for the visual effect. Just think—our website might be up by next week and ready for us to start taking reservations."

"And I've set the ad campaign to start. You'll be in the April issue of practically every ranch, outdoor living and vacation magazine. Not bad for two weeks' work."

"Not bad at all."

She tapped her phone again and stared at the screen. "Looks like we'll have to wait," she said, her disappointment obvious. "I'm so anxious to see the pictures."

John surveyed where they were on the trail. "Hey, our old tree house is around this curve. Why don't we see if you can catch a better signal up there?"

"In the tree house?"

He smiled. "You think we're too old for climbing into tree houses?"

"No…" The word was drawn out and sounded more like a question than an answer.

Then he realized that her vision of a tree house was probably altogether different from the masterpiece his father had designed when John was only six. "Don't worry. This isn't some ordinary tree house. This is Cutter carpentry at its finest."

"Really?" Her eyes sparkled with excitement, the way Abi's did on Christmas morning. She slid the phone back in her pocket. "Okay, show me this mansion of a tree house."

He led her around the curve where, sure enough, the massive structure still held residence in a towering oak tree.

"Wow, you weren't kidding, were you?"

"Nope," he said with pride.

"It doesn't look that old."

"That's because we keep adding on," he said with a laugh. "Landon and I added that skinny top section last summer when Abi wanted a lookout station. She said if the tree house was on Lookout Mountain, then it needed a special place where she could look out."

"She's adorable, isn't she?" Dana's fondness for Abi had been yet another quality that John admired. She obviously liked children, and his niece had developed quite a fondness for the city girl, too.

"Yeah, she is. I'll be glad when she gets back from Tampa."

"Me, too. I'd like to see her here. I'm sure she loves the tree house. I can't imagine anyone not liking it."

"If our guests take an interest in tree houses, we could add it as another dude ranch attraction. I'll need to make sure Casey puts it on the site."

Dana nodded. "And if Mandy didn't get any photos of it, let's ask her to come take some."

"I'll see if she can come back out one day this week.

Casey can go ahead and use what she's done so far, but a tree house picture should be on the site, too." He pointed to the wooden slats against the tree that served as a makeshift ladder. "That's the way up. You ready?"

She tilted her head to see the top, then moved her hand to the back of her cowboy hat to keep it from tumbling off. The tree house was high, and John began to wonder if perhaps she had a fear of heights.

"Still up for going in?"

"Yeah, but I've got to confess, I've never been in a tree house before. And the ones I've seen in photos haven't been this big, or this high."

"You've *never* been in a tree house?" John couldn't imagine a kid's life that didn't include a tree house.

"No. Never."

Okay, so she lived in the city. Probably not a lot of grass, much less a place for big trees and tree houses. "But you at least built some kind of fort every now and then, right? With chairs and sheets? Sat inside with a flashlight and told scary stories at night with your friends or with Ryan? Surely you had something similar to a tree house. I mean, you had Ryan, so he'd have helped you do stuff like that."

Her laugh rolled out. "Ryan and I building a fort? Can't even picture that, or what our housekeeper, Sylvia, would have done if we'd tried." Her mouth lifted on one side, and her shoulder followed suit in a minishrug. "I guess I had a deprived childhood, didn't I?"

He realized the absurdity of her statement as he thought about all her family's material possessions, but then, in the back of his mind, he thought, *Yeah, you did.* "Come on, then. You need to check this out. You're long overdue. I had some serious good times in this tree house." John grinned. "Landon and I spent time here hiding out from the bad guys." He nodded toward the first rungs on the tree. "You go ahead. I'll stay behind you in case you need any help."

She smiled. "Okay." Then she released his hand to start climbing the wooden planks, and John instantly missed the touch of her skin against his. He waited, let her get a couple of steps ahead, then followed, ready to help her if she stumbled along the way. The homemade rungs were steady enough, but the ridges weren't all that thick and he wanted to be there if her boots slipped. However, she had no trouble at all, climbing the makeshift ladder as though she'd been climbing into tree houses her entire life. What a shame that she hadn't.

"Oh, my!" Her exclamation came at the moment her head crested the floor of the tree house and she peeked inside. John knew exactly what she saw, hardwood forming the floor, walls and ceiling, windows that had burlap curtains and plaid tiebacks, courtesy of Eden, a small table and a wooden chest that, unless Abi had changed things, held an assortment of John and Landon's favorite books from when they were young. Other various "tools," primarily for kids—binoculars and telescopes and flashlights—as well as a few board games and decks of cards.

He waited until her boots disappeared inside and then followed her in.

She checked her phone. "No signal here, either."

"Guess we'll have to wait for town, after all," John

said, but neither of them made any move to leave. In fact, Dana wasted no time moving to the opposite wall and peeking out the window.

"John, come look at this. This view is amazing."

"I know." He joined her to look through the trees. It wasn't a view of the mountain itself, but more of the woods, the dogwood trees blooming stark white beneath the taller hardwoods, as well as patches of those vibrant rhododendrons offering bright splashes of color, like paint tossed from Heaven, across the forest.

"Mandy *has* to photograph this." Dana snapped several pictures with her phone. "And that artist in town— what was her name again?"

"Gina Brown?"

"Right. She should paint it. This is one of the most beautiful things I've ever seen."

Her admiration for the old tree house and the view it provided again reminded him of how much she truly enjoyed where he lived. The city girl loved the country. And John couldn't deny the truth any longer.

He loved the city girl.

She gazed out the window and sighed, her eyes blinking several times as she took it all in, and then her tears pushed free.

"Dana?"

Her mouth quivered, and those tears found paths down her cheeks and along her neck. He reached out and gently wiped them away, her skin soft and smooth against the pad of his thumb.

"My entire life, I remember my dad working hard so that we could have everything, do everything, see everything. He hardly enjoyed our time together, because he was always concentrating on how to get more, have more, do more. And all the trips and all of the gifts— none of those things were as beautiful as this." She pulled her gaze from the scene and focused intently, completely, on John. "And no one has ever made me *feel* like this, the way I feel here, with you. There's nothing fake, no thoughts of money or things, no opinions based on last names or prestige or anything. *That's* how I know this is different, that this is real. This feeling I have for you. I—" she shook her head "—I probably shouldn't be saying this now, and I don't even know if you feel the same…"

John couldn't let her finish. He'd held back on telling her how *he* felt, because of the situation. She was his investor. She was an affluent socialite. She was Dana Brooks, *the* Dana Brooks.

But emotions consumed him now, in the confines of the old tree house, with Dana looking at him with undeniable *love*.

He brushed her last tears away, and felt her tremble at his touch. "I can't deny that I'm falling for you, Dana." His mouth slid into a smile.

The corners of her mouth lifted.

But memories of MaciJo and the sting of losing her to the lure of the city pushed forward, and John wasn't sure if he could handle going down this road again. "But," he said, taking a deep breath, then easing it out, "you're going back to Chicago. Your life is there. And this is my home." He wanted Dana, wanted her more than anything he'd wanted for as long as he could remember, but he didn't want to give his heart only to have it broken again. "I don't want to start something here, pursuing our feelings and exactly how far this can go, and then have to watch you leave."

Honest, that was the only way he knew, and he couldn't bear to hand over his heart and then see her leave him behind. He cleared his throat, started to turn and head back down the tree house, and away from the woman he was fairly certain he loved.

"John." Her whisper was barely audible, but he stopped his progress. "Look at me, please."

He did as she asked, and his heart clenched in his chest as he saw the emotion in her eyes. Because she also had to see the reality. Their lives were separate, and they'd need to keep them separate now, so they wouldn't have the pain of breaking apart later. "We'll be okay," he said. "We can still work together, get the ranch going together. I just can't act on these feelings, because I've done that before, and I don't want to risk going through that again, Dana. I can't."

"I care about you, too, John."

John swallowed, her admission causing his heart to race. How would they work together each day knowing how they felt about each other?

"I love it here, and I honestly have no desire to go back," she said.

"What are you saying, Dana?" Though he thought— hoped—he knew.

She edged closer. "I'm saying that I don't think I want to leave. Ever."

John couldn't believe what he was hearing, but this

was no dream. The emotion in her eyes, in her heart—he felt it, saw it and believed it. He cradled her face in his hands, studied the exquisite woman who'd entered his world, won his heart and now said she wanted to stay in his life forever. Exactly where he wanted her. "You're sure?"

"Very, very sure." Her whisper feathered across his lips, and he lost himself in the tenderness of the moment. Their kiss was sweet and gentle, like the love they were finding one day at a time. The warmth of her embrace let him know that she wanted him as much as he wanted her, for the rest of their lives.

Chapter Eleven

Dana knew she needed to talk to Ryan about her new plans for the future. But every time he called, she chickened out. Plus, he was so much more interested in pointing out all the ways that the dude ranch didn't make the cut for an investment Brooks International should ever support.

The problem was, as much as Dana loved the farm and wanted the dude ranch to thrive, Ryan was right. In the past two weeks, ever since she'd managed to get insurance—and since she and John had admitted their feelings for each other—they'd completed the website, prepared the tent area, composed daily activities and schedules and advertised in every publication Dana could find, as well as the largest newspapers and radio stations across the Southeast. When that only yielded a few phone calls, and no reservations, Dana expanded her budget and extended her advertising to larger cities across the United States, thinking families in the bigger cities would find the change of pace a wonderful attraction for their summer vacation.

But still, not a single reservation.

And Ryan had viewed that fact as the final nail in the coffin for any future "high-risk, rags-to-riches investments," as he'd dubbed the ranch.

Dana prayed that a miracle would happen and that somehow people would see the beauty that this place had to offer. She really needed it to happen quickly, because she was supposed to go back to Chicago tomorrow. And she still hadn't told Ryan she didn't plan to get on the plane. Nor had she told John that she hadn't found the nerve to tell Ryan that she wanted to stay in Claremont.

"Hey, Miss Dana, are you still getting the tents ready? Because this is taking a lot longer than we thought, and I don't want to miss the fun things if you're doing something fun!" Abi's yell echoed through the woods, followed by John's laughter.

Dana finished rolling out Abi's sleeping bag, poked her head out of the tent the two would share tonight and answered, "I'm getting the sleeping bags ready, then I'm going to unpack the rest of the things in our tent, and then I'll do the same in your uncle John's tent. Nothing fun at all."

Again, she heard John's laugh, then his deep baritone as he told his niece, "Abi, we have to gather the sticks for the fire, or we can't roast the marshmallows and hot dogs."

Abi's response was muffled by the woods, but Dana could almost hear the child's typical, "Awww."

Smiling, she returned to the tent and prepared her own sleeping bag, laid out Abi's nightclothes so they'd be ready for later and tried to push her worries about the ranch's success out of her mind. She and John had basically planned their future, with the two of them running the dude ranch as well as finding additional types of start-up business investments across the country for this new arm of Brooks International to fund.

But if the ranch failed, there was no way the board would keep forking over money, especially not to the tune of the amount she'd spent for the dude ranch. And if she and John didn't have the dude ranch to run—plus working with Brooks International from here to get new start-up businesses up and running—then how could she justify moving? What would she tell Ryan?

God, I know You hear me. And I know that You can see the problems I'm facing and how much I want this to work. Help me figure out what to do. I can't completely walk away from the company Daddy built, the company he loved. But I also can't leave the ranch and the man I love. I know it's asking a lot, but if there's a way, can You let me do both?

A buzz sounded from the small duffel bag she'd packed with her things, and for a moment, she didn't recognize the sound of her phone. Gaining a cell signal in the woods was rare, and she rather liked the thing not going off all day long, the way it always had in Chicago. But now, since she hadn't answered a call in forever, she fished it out, saw Ryan's name and answered. "Hey."

"Well, you gave it a valiant effort, sis."

"What?"

"I'm looking at the neat little calendar for bookings that your web guy put on the dude ranch site. The site looks pretty sharp, by the way, for a kid to have done it."

"Casey is twenty, Ryan. He's hardly a kid."

"That's a kid in my book."

She didn't point out that Ryan was merely eight years older than the "kid."

"Anyway, from what I see, there isn't a single date booked with anyone. Unless there's a problem with the site and it doesn't actually show reservations on the calendar. Is that it? Is there a problem?"

He knew there wasn't, so Dana didn't answer.

"That's what I thought. I commend you on trying to help this country boy out, but you have to admit, it didn't work. I'm leaving for San Francisco Saturday and will be evaluating that Napa Valley property. But with the final details coming in on the Miami deal and the board's monthly meeting coming up, I need you back here."

"Ryan, I don't think I'm coming back," she started, then couldn't keep herself from adding, "yet."

He paused a beat then she heard him exhale thickly through the line. "What do you mean, you aren't coming back yet?"

"We've still got a lot going on down here." That was true. She and John were finally taking Abi camping, and the city's First Friday celebration for the month of April would happen next week. Apparently, they had a festival on the first Friday of every month at the town square with local artists and vendors entertaining the community. She'd looked forward to it ever since John mentioned it. Truthfully, she looked forward to everything Claremont had to offer. And she looked forward to experiencing it all with John.

"Dana, the gala at the Art Institute is Tuesday night. And you can't have that much going on down there. You told me the place was up and ready to go last week. There's no reason for you to stay, and there's no way you can cancel on the presentation of the Brooks wing at the Institute. They already have it on their website that you're attending, and they've advertised around the city."

"You could go," she said, even though she knew that wasn't an option. He was due to be in California, and she'd committed to the event. And their father would have wanted one of them there for the presentation; Lawrence Brooks had been a big supporter of the Art Institute, even though Ryan didn't agree with their father about donating so much money to something that didn't yield a profit. He didn't appreciate the beauty of the Institute the way Dana and their father did. Dana took after their father that way, appreciating the beauty of unique things. She glanced toward the creek, glistening with a hint of gold as it reflected the setting sun. Then she looked toward the waterfall in the distance, and the dogwoods blooming, and the trees in endless shades of green. This was more beautiful than any painting or structure she'd ever seen at the Institute, or anywhere else.

"Dana, I can't go. You said you would, and William Montgomery is looking forward to escorting you to the event."

She didn't want to ask how Ryan knew William looked forward to it. They were probably still golfing together, still lunching together, still planning a joint future for Montgomery Incorporated and Brooks International. But it didn't matter; her future would be here, one way or another. However, she didn't see a way out of attending the art event. So she'd go back, attend the gala and then find her way back to Claremont. And back to John. "Okay, I'll go."

"Good. I'll have the plane there early tomorrow morning. I'd like a chance to talk to you before I leave town and fill you in on everything that's been happening here while you've been gone."

"No, I'll call and let them know when I'm ready to go. I have a few things to take care of here before I leave." Like telling John that she was going back to Chicago, but also promising him—and praying he believed—that she'd return.

"Miss Dana, we got the sticks! Are you ready to cook marshmallows and hot dogs?" Abi ran toward the campsite.

"I've got to go, Ryan."

"Are you *camping?*"

"Yes, I'm camping—testing the ranch's campsites."

"You went down there to invest *our* company's money in a profit-making business. That hasn't happened, and I'm not sure what's going on there, but you need to come back and get back to real life."

John walked toward the campsite with his arms filled

with wood for the fire. He winked at Dana, sending her heart racing and her mind planning all the wonderful days that she looked forward to spending with this man. She held up a finger to John, then moved back into the tent and whispered to her brother, "Ryan, *you* don't understand. I am happy here. I love it here. And if I didn't have to come home for that gala, I don't think I'd ever leave."

"Dana, you aren't thinking—"

She disconnected, turned off the phone and climbed back out of the tent. "Ready to cook some hot dogs?"

John always thought Dana looked beautiful, but tonight, in the glow of a campfire with Abi sitting on her lap, she was mesmerizing. Abi had wanted to roast one more round of marshmallows before she went to bed, but her heavy eyes were taking some very long blinks. Consequently, Dana had to help her roast the treat by holding Abi's tired wrist as she held the stick toward the flame.

"Are you sure you want to eat another one? We'll do this again another time," he said to his sleepy niece. "You don't have to stay up all night."

She yawned, blinked and rested her head against Dana's shoulder. "I—I guess I can go to bed." Then she lifted her head a little and squinted at Dana. "I'm too tired to eat the last one, anyway."

"That's okay," John said. "I'll take care of that for you." He took the stick from Dana, carefully slid the hot marshmallow off the end and held it toward Abi. "Sure you don't want it?"

"No, too tired," she said, yawning again. "Maybe for breakfast."

John laughed at that, then popped the marshmallow in his mouth and leaned over Dana, still sitting on a sideways log and holding his exhausted niece. "Here, I'll carry her to the tent."

Abi blinked a couple of times as John eased her out of Dana's arms and into his own. "Are you coming to bed, too, Miss Dana?" The tiny hint of panic told John that Abi didn't want to sleep on her own.

"Yes, I'll be there soon," Dana assured.

"But—" another wide yawn "—you can come say prayers now, right? With me and Uncle John? And tuck me in?"

Dana blinked, swallowed. "Yes, I'd like that very much."

She stood and followed John to the small tent he'd set up for Dana and Abi to share. Then the three of them crawled inside, and Abi shimmied into her sleeping bag. Her eyes were still heavy, but she wasn't surrendering to the pull of sleep until she said her prayers. The importance of her nightly ritual touched John's heart, as did the fact that she'd wanted both John and Dana to be a part of it tonight.

"Okay," he said. "You want to go first?"

"Sure." She closed her eyes. "Dear God, thank You for letting the rain stop and letting us finally go camping." A big yawn. "And—and thank You for letting us have a dude ranch. And thank You for letting Miss Dana come and for her being Uncle John's girlfriend. And thank You for them loving me." She yawned once more, the biggest yawn yet. "Night, night, God. I love You. Amen."

John could barely see Dana in the faint moonlight spilling in through the tent, but even in shadow, he could tell she was touched by Abi's prayer. "You want to go next?"

She nodded. Then she waited a couple of seconds before starting. "Dear God, thank You for letting me find the ranch and the Cutter family. Thank You for blessing me so much and showing me what's really important. I love You, too. Amen."

John reached out, found her hand and held it as he prayed, "Dear Lord, we love You and we praise You. You have a mighty plan, and I am grateful that You brought Dana into our lives and into our hearts. Thank You for her desire to be a part of our lives forever." He silently added, *thank You for her desire to be a part of my life forever, Lord. And bless our lives together, always.* "In Your Son's holy name, Amen."

Abi's low snore had started before John completed his prayer, and he chuckled as he tucked her sleeping bag under her chin and then kissed her cheek. Dana also moved toward the sleeping child and kissed her cheek before following John back out of the tent.

They sat on the log by the firelight, John wrapping an arm around her and pulling her close. "She does love you," he said, touched that Dana had so quickly earned such a prominent place in Abi's heart.

"I love her, too." She snuggled closer against him, and John relished this quiet time together. He'd enjoyed hiking with Abi up the mountain and setting up the camp, and Georgiana and Landon had been excited about having a night to themselves while knowing their little girl was having a good time with John and Dana, but John had also looked forward to the time after Abi went to sleep, time he could be completely alone with Dana. They had so much to talk about, so much to plan for their future together. And because of the lack of interest in the dude ranch, John wasn't certain how to prepare at all.

"Abi has been so excited about the dude ranch, and she's still planning to teach the kids how to ride." He couldn't disguise the sadness in his tone. He'd had such high hopes, and so had Dana. "Have you talked to Ryan, or any of the other board members?"

She nodded, but kept her focus on the fire, dying down slowly and causing the last bit of firelight to fade.

"I don't suppose they'll be apt to fund any additional projects like this unless something changes and we start booking reservations." The statement didn't require a response. He knew the answer and, obviously, so did she, because she didn't say a word. But a glance at her face caused John to see her disappointment, when a thick tear caught the moonlight and slid slowly down her cheek.

"I'm going to take another look at our advertising, the website, the ranch itself, over the next few days and see if there's something we're missing. Maybe we aren't targeting the right audience." He racked his brain to remember everything he'd learned in his business classes at the university. But he knew the reality; Dana had some of the most capable advertising agents available through Brooks International, and she'd used them to generate the campaign that presumably cost a small fortune. And John didn't have a single reservation on the books.

"Yeah, maybe we've missed something," she whispered, but the optimism he'd grown accustomed to hearing each time she spoke was gone. She'd started to give up on the ranch, and John prayed that she hadn't started giving up on him. He had to make the ranch work somehow. There had to be some hook, some marketing tool, that the experts had missed. Surely.

He ran a hand up and down her arm, trying to provide the comfort he knew she needed. He'd work things out for her, make this investment turn into a good thing, one way or another. He couldn't let her fail because of him.

"I need to tell you something." Her voice was hesitant, nervous.

John's stomach tightened. "Okay."

"That call I got earlier in the tent—it was Ryan. And he reminded me of some obligations I have in Chicago—" she paused "—next week."

John's hand stopped moving against her arm, his throat tightened so much he wasn't sure he could swallow. She wasn't staying. She was heading back to Chicago. Leaving the country for the city, because he didn't have anything to offer her here.

"I will come back," she quickly added, "as soon as I can."

"Right." He couldn't bear to look at her, so he kept his attention focused on the last embers on the fire, dying steadily as he watched. Odd how something so alive, so exhilarating, one minute could so quickly turn to ash the next.

Chapter Twelve

John attempted to be cordial to the woman he loved as they packed up the camp this morning and hiked back, but his effort at manners was futile with the realization that she was going back to Chicago. He'd had such high hopes for the dude ranch and had already started picturing the two of them running the place together, having a successful business and also assisting other would-be entrepreneurs in doing the same. Dana could oversee that part of Brooks International while living on the farm with John, being married to John, spending many nights camping together with her holding a child in her arms the way she'd held Abi last night. Except the child would be theirs. In his vision, the ranch thrived. And Dana didn't feel as though she were missing out by spending her life with an Alabama rancher.

But the dude ranch hadn't panned out. And John would be lying if he said he had anything worthy to offer her if she moved here. He didn't want to live off her inheritance, wouldn't be seen as a charity case for the heiress who'd been unfortunate enough to lose her heart to the broke cowboy from the sticks. He wanted to be worthy of her love, and he would be. He simply had to figure out how.

He'd been at the cabin less than an hour after leaving Abi and Dana at the main house when his phone rang, the screen displaying a Chicago number. Not Dana's number, but the same area code. "Hello."

"Is this John Cutter?" The guy sounded anxious.

"Yes."

"This is Ryan Brooks. I've been trying to reach Dana all morning and can't get her to answer her phone. Is she with you?"

"No, but I can get her a message. Her phone should work now, though, because we got in from the mountain over an hour ago. Have you tried her in the past hour?"

"Repeatedly."

Obviously, Dana didn't want to talk to her brother, but John felt obligated to at least relay the fact that the guy was trying so hard to reach her. "Well, as I said, I can get her a message."

"Yes, if you'd do that, I'd appreciate it." He paused. "I texted her, too. Do you get texts there?"

John tried not to respond sarcastically to the insulting question. This was Dana's brother, and if John had his way, eventually, Ryan Brooks would be his brother-in-law. "Yes, we get texts."

"Then she may know already, but in any case, her plane is waiting for her at the landing strip in Stockville."

John felt as if he'd been punched straight to the gut.

"She's leaving this morning?" He wasn't really asking, merely stating the fact so that his heart could process the reality.

"She'd better be. She told me she'd watch over things here while I'm away next week. And she's representing our company at the Art Institute's grand opening of our father's wing on Tuesday." He paused a couple of beats, then added, "She told me last night that she was still attending the gala with William."

"William?"

"William Montgomery, the guy she's dating here."

Another sucker punch, but John swallowed through the shock. "I'll make sure she gets to the plane."

Within minutes, he'd saddled Red and started back toward the house, where he found several suitcases on the front porch, and Abi sitting on the front steps with her head in her hands. Usually, she'd stand and run toward John as he approached, but this time, she merely sat there looking defeated.

John left Red in the barn and then gathered his courage before starting to the house. He had to hold it all together for Abi, and for Dana.

"There's my newest camper. Did you tell your folks about how much fun we had?"

She sniffed, wiped at both of her eyes. "Yeah, but then Miss Dana told me she had to go back to Chicago today, and now I'm sad."

He knew exactly how she felt. Dropping beside her on the step, he tugged at a pigtail. "It'll be okay." His words were spoken to his precious niece, but the sentiment was directed specifically to his heart.

The front door of the house creaked as it opened, and John turned to see Georgiana and Dana each carrying a small piece of luggage. "Is that the last of it?" he asked, not missing Dana's wet cheeks and trembling mouth.

"Oh, John, I didn't know you were here. Dana heard from her brother this morning…"

"I know. I heard from him, too."

Dana's head shook. "I'm sorry about that. I was going to come down to the cabin and tell you myself, but I didn't know he'd send the plane this early, and then he texted again telling me you were on your way to take me to the airport."

"It's okay." John again directed the words not only to the stunning city girl, but also to his heart. "I'll load your bags in the truck."

Then he gave Abi a quick kiss on the forehead, grabbed a couple of the larger pieces of luggage and somehow managed to keep his composure while putting all of Dana's things in the bed of his truck. The three females were quiet on the porch as he loaded the remainder of her bags, then Abi's sobs broke free as she stood and wrapped her arms around Dana.

"You said you wanted to stay here forever. That's what you told me." Abi's heartfelt words made John's heart clench.

"I know, sweetie," Dana said. "And I meant what I said, but I—I have to go back home to take care of some things."

"So you'll come back? After you take care of everything?"

Dana glanced at John. "I want to."

Abi swiped at her cheeks again. "Don't wait too long. I'm going to miss you, and Uncle John will miss you, too."

That was a major understatement.

"I'll miss all of you." Dana stepped toward Georgiana, hugged her. "Tell Landon I'm sorry I didn't get to see him before I left, but I had no idea I'd be leaving so early this morning."

"I'll tell him."

"And thank you for letting me stay with all of you. I can't say how wonderful it's been."

"We wouldn't have had it any other way."

Dana gave Abi another hug. "Love you, Abi."

"I love you, Miss Dana."

Then she turned toward John. "I guess I'm ready."

He nodded, walked ahead of her toward the truck and opened her door. Then he fought against the pull of her sweet scent as she eased past him and sat inside. Circling the cab, he got behind the wheel and started the truck, then began driving the pretty city girl away from the farm the same way he had so many times over the past four weeks. But this time, he wasn't taking her to church, or to the town square, or to the coffeehouse in Stockville, or to any of the other places they'd visited together. And this time, they wouldn't be returning to the farm, laughing and chatting about their journey and about the differences between his small town and her big city. This time he wouldn't bring her back at all.

"It'll be okay," he repeated, more to himself than to the woman in his passenger seat.

Her hand moved on top of his on the gearshift,

and she gently squeezed. "Will it, John? Because you haven't been the same since I said I needed to go back for a few days. I told Abi the truth. I want to come back here. And I told you the truth. I want to live here forever, with you."

John rounded a curve and focused on what to say. He could tell her that was fine, for her to do whatever she needed to do in Chicago and then return, and they could live off her fortune the rest of their lives.

And he could feel like a complete failure, the rest of his life.

But he couldn't—wouldn't—do that.

"I don't want you to come back, Dana."

"You don't?"

He continued driving, knew they would reach the airport fairly quickly and didn't want to leave anything unsaid, and he needed her to understand his feelings before she got on that plane. "The dude ranch hasn't made it, and I get that. I'm not sure if I can make it work or not, but I realize that our first effort at making it happen failed. And I also know that I can't support you with what I'm making now."

"I don't need…"

He shook his head. "Hear me out. I know you don't need me to support you when it comes to the two of us being together long term, but I need it. I would never feel good about myself, would never feel worthy of you, if I didn't somehow make a living on my own. Not just scraping by but really providing for my family."

"So—" she looked up as the landing strip came into view, a shiny white plane parked at one end with Brooks

International written across the side in navy and gold "—so are you saying that we can't have a relationship at all? Because that's not what I want, John. I love you."

Have mercy, she was making this hard, but John couldn't budge on this. He had to feel worthy of her love. "I love you, too, more than you could possibly realize." He couldn't imagine living without her, didn't know if he could breathe without her. "But I can't live like that, feeling that I'm not good enough. I—won't."

"But then, what about us? Is it—are we over?"

"I need time, Dana. Time to figure out if I can make the dude ranch work, or to see if I can make something else work. And if I can't, if I'm meant to work two or three jobs the rest of my life and just scrape by, then so be it, but I won't make you live that way."

"What if I want to live whatever way I can, to be with you?"

"You've got obligations in Chicago. You have *people* who are important to you there, and you should go and take care of that part of your life. And while you do, I'll see what kind of a life I can have here, and whether I can be everything you need."

"*People* important to me? You mean Ryan?"

John pulled up to the plane, where two guys he presumed were the pilots stood nearby. "Ryan, and William…" He let the last name draw out, and then wished he had been able to keep it to himself.

She twisted in the seat to face him. "Ryan shouldn't have told you about William."

"No, *you* should have."

"He's an acquaintance, John. That's all."

"An acquaintance who you have a date with next week, according to your brother." John had never been jealous, not one day in his entire life. Until now. And he didn't make an effort to hide the green emotion from Dana. He'd been honest with her about all his other pitfalls, might as well throw this emotion out there, too.

"It isn't a date," she said. "He's escorting me to an event."

"Down here in the country we call that a date," he said, as one of the pilot guys opened the passenger door.

"Hello, Ms. Brooks. Are you ready to start back home?" His smile slipped a little when he saw Dana's tears.

"Yes, Ned, I am."

"I'll get your things moved over to the plane." He nodded toward John and then moved to the back of the truck and began removing her luggage.

"I'll go help him with your luggage." John started to open the door, but stopped when she reached for his arm.

"John."

He took a deep breath, exhaled and turned to face her. "Yeah?"

"William doesn't mean anything to me."

He closed his eyes, said a quick prayer for strength.

"I want to make sure you believe that," she added.

"The thing is, I do believe it, Dana. I believe that he doesn't mean anything to you, or you would have told me about him. I've come to know you well enough to realize that. But the thing is, even if he doesn't mean anything to you, he—and every guy like him—means a lot to me. Because he shows me everything that you deserve, and everything that I can't provide."

Chapter Thirteen

John climbed out of the truck and slammed the door hard enough for the entire vehicle to rattle. Then he turned, leaned his head against the side and closed his eyes.

Lord, I need Your help here. I don't know what to do. I don't know how to make this work, make the ranch work, so that I can feel like I have something to offer Dana. I want her here, Lord, but I need to be able to provide for her if she's willing to move here for me. Show me, God. Help me know what to do.

"You realize that ol' truck is gonna give up the ghost just to spite you if you keep treating it that way."

John opened his eyes to see Landon slapping his work gloves together and sending bits of dirt sifting through the sunshine in the process. He'd obviously already unloaded all the feed and hay from the feed store. With Dana's sudden departure, John had forgotten to help him out. "This truck will hold its own, I reckon, like its owner." He tilted his head toward the barn. "I forgot about the feed run."

"Not a problem. Figured you had other things on your mind." Landon wiped the sweat from his forehead with the back of his hand. "You want to talk about it, or not?"

"Not."

His brother nodded as though he expected that answer. "What about a ride? Red looks ready, and Sam's feeling good as new again. Want to take them across the ridge?"

"Now you're talking."

They didn't say a word as they saddled the horses and rode across the fields and toward the mountains. Sam and Red seemed to sense the brothers' need for a stress-reliever, because, though they both were well past their prime, they galloped the familiar route as though they were yearlings again. Free and without a care in the world, ready to run—and run fast.

John had plenty of cares in the world right now, more than he could ever remember having before, even after his mother had died and he'd been left to raise Casey. Because he'd found the girl of his dreams, his soul mate, and he'd lost her.

For now.

By the time he and Landon crested the ridge and the horses had slowed to a walk, the tension in his muscles had subsided, his heart had released the frustration at knowing another man would escort Dana to a gala next week and his mind had started contemplating exactly what he could do to make the dude ranch profitable. And get back the woman he loved.

Sam nickered, and Landon stroked her neck. "She wants water. Let's head down to the Sanders's pond and let them drink."

"Red wouldn't mind a drink, I'm sure. It's been a while since he's been ridden this hard." He and Red followed Landon and Sam down the ridge toward Eden Sanders's ranch, an exact replica of the Cutter property with a big two-story log home in the center surrounded by fields and ponds, cattle and horses, and a large Mennonite barn. The only difference was where the Cutter barn was red, the Sanders barn was forest-green. Georgiana had been raised on this farm, and the three of them had spent many years riding the trails, the ridge and the fields together, enjoying the natural beauty of God's country.

John followed Landon to the pond, then they let the horses drink their fill, while he wondered about Dana's childhood. She undoubtedly hadn't spent her time finding simple ways to entertain herself, like building forts or skipping stones or riding the trails. She hadn't mentioned any friends from childhood; in fact, the only friends she'd mentioned during the entire time she'd been on the ranch had been her sorority sisters from college. And she'd said they hardly spoke anymore, since everyone had gone their separate ways after graduation.

The only family she had was a brother who was more interested in work than in enjoying life and who didn't appear to have much of a faith system at all, from what John could determine. Ryan sounded like a bowto-the-almighty-dollar kind of city guy that John had never understood.

He thought of William, the guy who'd be escorting Dana next week. He felt fairly certain the man was probably a lot like Ryan, and he'd told Dana the truth when he said he believed she wasn't interested in the city boy. In fact, he knew she wasn't.

She loved John.

But John had to find a way to show her that he could take care of her in every way. He just had to determine how.

"Sometimes I still can't believe how lucky we are to live in the middle of all this." Landon's statement caused John to survey his surroundings again. Shades of green cloaked the mountains with patches of white and vibrant color interspersed with blooming foliage. Rolling fields stretched out as far as John could see. A dozen or so huge round hay bales were sporadically left around the fields, a result of yesterday's hay baling. A large stocked pond held an abundance of crappie, bream and catfish; one overzealous fish splashed completely out of the water while John scanned the slick surface.

Landon was right, they were lucky to live here surrounded by all this beauty. And the only thing that would make it more beautiful would be to have Dana by his side.

"I've got to find a way to bring her back."

Landon didn't have to ask who he was talking about. "From what Georgiana told me this morning, all you have to do is ask. Dana doesn't want to stay away, she likes it here. And I'd thought the two of you had decided to make this relationship something permanent, with her here in Alabama. I mean, it sure looked that way to me."

"That was when I thought the dude ranch would make it. I can't bring her here if I have to live off her inheritance." When Landon raised a brow, John added, "Okay, I could, but I won't."

"Nah, I couldn't do it, either. Maybe it's because we've fought so hard to hang on to the farm through the tough times and don't want to use someone else's money to help us out now. But for some reason, I'm not all that keen on Dana riding in to save the day, either."

John grinned. "I don't think that's what she was trying to do."

"I know, but you get what I'm saying. We should be able to figure this thing out—the dude ranch, I mean. It's a great idea for a vacation. Why aren't people seeing it?"

"I have no idea. We've advertised it everywhere, and we've got the place ready to go, but we still don't have anything on the books." He shook his head. "And I'm not sure what else to try."

Sam nickered, and Red followed suit. Then several other horses in the field joined in, as though they were speaking their own language. John and Landon exchanged bemused looks.

"What do you think got into all of them?" John scanned the field to see if something had spooked them, but then again, they were nickering happily, nothing like the noise they'd make if they were scared.

Landon laughed. "Well, maybe they're trying to tell

us what to do about the dude ranch, and we just can't speak their language."

John smiled. "Maybe so."

The horses continued the odd behavior, and John's memory latched onto the prayer he'd said a short while ago, where he asked God to help him know what to do.

And then he had it.

Thank you, Lord.

"Hey, I'm going to head on back. I've got an idea."

Landon's brows lifted. "From the horses?"

"Pretty much. I need to go see Brother Henry, though, to see if what I'm thinking might work. You want to ride back with me?"

"Nah, Abi's got her riding lesson over here with Eden in an hour. I'm going to wait and watch her." He laughed again at the horses, still nickering. "So, they're telling you something? You going to let me in on what?"

"After I talk to Brother Henry." John took another glance at all the horses in the field that seemed to be urging him on. Then he rode Red back to the ranch, quickly moved to the truck and, in less than twenty minutes, he entered Brother Henry's office.

The preacher looked up from his Bible and nodded. "Isn't that something?" He almost acted as though he expected John's visit.

"Isn't what something?" John asked, pleased that they had such a good relationship that he could merely enter the preacher's office and launch right into a conversation.

"We just finished a prayer for you and for your sweet Dana, and then you walked in my door."

"We?" John sat in one of the guest chairs near the preacher's desk.

"Me and Mary. She stepped out to go get us some coffee from the kitchen."

"You were praying for us—me and Dana?"

He nodded. "Georgiana called Mary a short while ago and asked us to pray for the two of you, so we did. And then you walk through the door. I'm assuming God sent you here?"

"I reckon He did."

The preacher's wife entered, carrying two steaming mugs, glanced at John and beamed. "Why, we just prayed for you."

"So I hear." John thought about what it'd be like to have a wife who would pray with him, be with him, make him smile, bring him coffee. Love him for the rest of his life, the way he would love her.

"Would you like me to get you a cup?" Mary gave Brother Henry his mug, and the preacher thanked her with a smile.

"No, thank you," John said, while Mary sat in the other guest chair and sipped her coffee.

"Okay if I stay while you two talk?" she asked.

"Yes," John said. "Because I really got this idea from you."

"What idea is that?"

"You remember when you told me about the Vacation Bible School program where you taught the kids about animals in the Bible, specifically horses?"

"Yes, of course. I actually saw all that material yesterday when I reorganized the supply room."

"We've tried to advertise our dude ranch to families who might consider it for a vacation, and we've had hardly any interest at all. But then I got to thinking that maybe we should target a different audience, and since our dude ranch would revolve around the horses—" he pictured all the horses nickering at him in the field "—I thought we could have a daily Bible study as part of the ranch activities."

"And your Bible study would focus on the verses in the Bible dealing with horses, the way our Bible school material did."

"Yes. In fact, I thought we could stop focusing our advertising on the magazines and newspapers where we try to target families and instead advertise to churches who might consider bringing their youth groups to a dude ranch for a youth retreat."

Brother Henry clapped his hands together. "John, that's an excellent idea."

"Yes," Mary joined in. "Churches are always looking for an unusual, fun activity that they can offer their youth, especially one that teaches the kids about the Bible. Plus, the children would love it. I've never met a child yet who doesn't like horses, or learning about them, for that matter." She stood. "I'll go get the material from the supply room."

"And I can do something for you, too," said Brother Henry, as he turned his chair to face his computer and tapped at the keyboard. "But I'd need to know how soon you'll be ready to get this going."

"As soon as I get that material from Mary, I'll work nonstop to get the new schedule of activities up to include horses in the Bible and promote the daily Bible studies, things that the churches would find appealing for their youth programs. I'm sure Landon, Georgiana, Abi and Eden will help. Casey could add the new info to the site this week to show that we're offering youth retreats now." John considered what all they needed to do. "I suppose we could start booking retreats as early as the week after next."

"Well, all right, then." Brother Henry continued typing and smiling. "I guess it'll be okay for me to send an announcement about this new youth retreat opportunity to all my Christian youth groups online, don't you think? Tell them to check the website out this week and let them know that they can start making their reservations as early as two weeks from now. Sound good?"

John's ears perked up, and he could feel a tiny surge of adrenaline in his veins. "Brother Henry, exactly how many Christian youth groups are you connected to online?"

The preacher smiled, and winked. "Oh, about a hundred, maybe more."

The adrenaline picked it up another notch. "You aren't joking?"

"I wouldn't joke with you about something this big. It's a great idea, John. God-inspired, I'd say."

He again pictured all those horses nickering in the field. "Definitely God-inspired."

"So it's okay for me to send this out? Tell them to check the site each day while you're getting everything up and rolling, and then start booking their youth retreats?"

"Yes, it's okay, more than okay." John laughed at the rapid turn of events, all orchestrated undeniably by God. And then he smiled. Soon churches would fill his reservation calendar with youth retreats. And soon, he'd show Dana how he could make a business work on his own, and how he could provide for his future bride… on his own.

Chapter Fourteen

Dana turned her office chair away from her desk and toward the floor-to-ceiling windows that offered an incomparable view of Chicago and Lake Michigan. That's how the panorama from the Brooks International executive offices had been described. But Dana didn't see the scene as compelling anymore. It didn't capture her imagination like a waterfall in the woods; make her wonder what surprises were hidden in the landscape like vivid purple, pink and red rhododendrons; cause her to think about God and the natural beauty that He alone created.

The beauty she'd fallen in love with on the ranch.

She turned toward the framed photo she'd ordered from Mandy Brantley, the picture taken from the tree house window. Mandy had caught the endless shades of green throughout the trees, the pristine white blooms of the dogwoods in the distance, the brilliant jewel tones of the rhododendrons. The first time Dana had viewed that scene had been just before she confessed her feelings to John.

She missed him terribly. He'd called her daily since she left two weeks ago and told her that he was still working to promote the dude ranch, still hopeful that everything would work out and that the Brooks International board would eventually be proud of their decision to invest in his venture. *Then* he said he'd feel as though he had something to offer Dana. *Then* he'd want her to live with him on the farm for good.

Dana's biggest fear was that *then* would never come. She had done everything she knew how to make the dude ranch succeed, and nothing had worked. On top of that, her advertising geniuses had utilized a multimedia campaign, targeting peak markets for the ranch.

And still…nothing.

But John sounded so optimistic every time they talked, as if he had a plan and that it would work. However, he never shared his idea, nor did he say how long he thought it would take to accomplish his goal. Dana prayed he succeeded, and she also prayed that it wouldn't take long.

But today, unfortunately, the dude ranch investment, as well as future similar investments, was on the board meeting's agenda. And they wanted her to present an update on the endeavor.

Dana had no desire to inform the group that the project had failed.

Her phone rang. She glanced at the display, saw her brother's name and answered. She'd known he would call; the board meeting was scheduled to begin in fifteen minutes, and he wanted her there. But he'd have to keep wanting.

She didn't wait for him to say hello. "Ryan, I'm not going. If they want a presentation about the ranch, you can do it. You're the only one happy about the outcome, after all."

"No, you're wrong. I'm not happy about it, not at all."

"You're not?" She found that hard to believe. Ryan had shot down the dude ranch from day one, had sent that plane well before she was ready to leave and hadn't held back on his skepticism toward her undertaking.

"Do you think I like seeing you mope around here every day? Acting like you'd rather be anywhere but here and doing things I don't understand, like redecorating your office the way you have?"

She'd only added two things to the office. "I hung a photograph and a painting, Ryan. That's hardly redecorating."

"Did you have to get them both so large?"

She'd ordered the biggest size possible of Mandy's photo and the largest canvas painting Gina Brown had available. She took her attention from Mandy's photo of the woods to the painting of the charming white church. She so missed all the members at Claremont Community Church, and she wondered if they missed her, too. She thought about how close she'd gotten to several of the church members already and how they were all like a family, taking care of each other through good times and bad. She remembered that afternoon in the kitchen with Georgiana, Eden and Abi cooking meals for Mitch Gillespie.

"You know what, Ryan?"

"What?"

"When Daddy passed away, no one brought a casserole."

The other end of the line went silent, and she imagined Ryan counting to ten. Then he must have finished, because finally, he spoke. "Dana, we don't even eat casseroles. What are you talking about?"

"I love casseroles." She sniffed. "I miss casseroles."

He groaned. "I have no idea what they did to you down there, but you've changed."

"I know."

"I see it in the way you act, hear it in your voice. *Y'all* is not a word."

"Yes, it is."

"And the way you've been dressing for the office…"

She glanced down at her clothes. "What's wrong with the way I dress?"

The door to her office clicked as it opened. "Nothing at all. I especially like the boots."

Dana knew that voice, but she'd never dreamed he would come here. She whirled around so fast she nearly lost her balance. "John."

Ryan chuckled. "Ah, so I see he made it in time. Good deal. Tell him I'll see him in the boardroom."

She couldn't believe what she was seeing. John, here in Chicago, in her office, no less. And then she realized what her brother had said on the other end of the line. "Ryan?"

"I love you, sis. And he loves you, too. He can tell

you what's going on, and you two can visit for a few minutes, but then we need both of you in the boardroom. ASAP." He disconnected, and Dana dropped the phone on her desk then crossed the room and jumped into her cowboy's arms.

"What are you doing—" she started, but he cut off her words with his kiss. He kissed her with sweet softness, as though he treasured her completely. And she knew that he did, the way she treasured him.

"I've missed you so much." He drew her against him and squeezed. "You have no idea."

"Yes, I do." She laughed against his chest. "I haven't stopped thinking about you, not one moment."

He did a quick survey of her office, focusing on the monstrous painting and the equally gigantic photo she'd had shipped to Chicago to remind her of Claremont, then he glanced down at the blue dress she'd bought from Maribeth, the same dress she'd worn the first time they went to church together, and then he ended his perusal by grinning down at the pink cowboy boots. "Not worried about blending with your fellow city folks here, are you?"

She smiled. "Not at all. I'd rather blend with the folks I love."

"That's what I'm talking about." He kissed her again.

Suddenly, a knock sounded at the door. Ryan poked his head in. "We're meeting in the boardroom in five minutes. You're ready, right?"

"I'm ready," John said.

"Ready for what?" she asked.

"To show them how successful their first rags-to-riches endeavor is. The calendar is filled from now until the end of September with about fifty more on our waiting list."

Her mouth fell open. "It's—what?"

"Thanks to Brother Henry." John shook his head. "Or rather, thanks to God. Church youth retreats, *that's* what set everything in motion. Remember when Brother Henry's wife talked about the Vacation Bible School and the lessons about horses? All the times they're mentioned in the Bible?"

"Yes," she said, then put it together. "Youth retreats! Places for church groups to go and spend time with horses while they're learning how horses figured in the Bible."

"That's it."

"How did you get the word out to the youth groups?"

"Brother Henry has quite a network with church groups online, so basically a few emails and phone calls, and we had reservations coming in by the hour. And it didn't cost a thing."

Dana had started believing in the power of prayer, but right here, right now, she could *see* the results of their prayers. Church youth groups would fill the ranch, an answer to John's prayer that the ranch be successful. And John was here, in Chicago, and ready to begin their life together, no doubt. Take her back to Claremont, back to the place and the people she loved, an answer to her own prayers. "That's wonderful, absolutely wonderful!"

"Yeah, it is, but it isn't the best part." He'd been wearing his Stetson, but he took it off, and Dana got the full effect of those amber eyes, and the trademark Cutter dimples that left her knees weak.

She swallowed. "So, if that isn't the best part, then what is?"

Never taking his eyes from hers, he slowly lowered himself onto one knee then withdrew a small black box from the pocket of his jeans. "This was my great-grandmother's," he said, opening the box to reveal an intricate antique engagement ring. "It isn't that big of a stone, but the jeweler said it's still great quality." He smiled. "Kind of like the rancher offering it to you. I don't have anything big to give you, Dana. Not a ton of money or material things. But I can take care of you, support you spiritually, emotionally and physically, for the rest of your life. If you'll let me."

She moved her finger toward the ring, cried as he slid it on her finger. "I don't want anything big and meaningless. I want the ring that means something to your family, and I want the only man who has ever meant anything to me. I love you, John."

A brief knock rapped on the door then Ryan stuck his head in once again. "Hey, it's time for—" he looked at John on one knee, Dana crying and beaming at the ring on her finger. "You asked her already? I thought you were going to wait until after the board meeting."

"I couldn't wait," John said, then stood and wrapped an arm around his brand-new fiancée.

"You knew?" Dana asked her brother.

"Well, of course. He asked me for your hand." He lifted a brow. "You can thank me later for saying he could have it. I really didn't know what choice I had, since you've been making everyone miserable in the office ever since you got back. And those boots…"

She held up a pink boot-clad foot. "What about them?"

"Just glad they're finding their way home." He looked from Dana to John. "And just so you know, I *am* glad the dude ranch took off. I didn't expect it, and wasn't sure I wanted it, but seeing Dana this happy, and knowing that we can continue helping other people like John—and like our Dad—make it in business, well, I can see how good a thing that is now."

Dana left John's embrace, crossed the room and hugged her brother. "Thanks, Ryan."

"You can thank me after John makes his presentation in the boardroom. Those guys get tired of waiting, you know. And speaking of waiting, how long are you two going to wait before tying the knot?"

"How does June sound?" John asked. "That long enough for you to get ready?"

"Yes," she whispered. "June sounds great."

"And I assume you'll want to get married down there," Ryan said.

"Definitely," Dana answered.

"Guess I've got a trip to the sticks to look forward to in the near future."

"You'd be surprised at the things you find in the sticks." John moved toward Dana and wrapped an arm around her again. It felt so good to be able to touch her, hold her, tell her that he loved her and would love her forever. He kissed her cheek. "Isn't that right?"

She smiled up at him, blue eyes filled with love. "Yes," she whispered, "that's right."

Epilogue

W hile the paparazzi hadn't found it necessary to follow Dana to Alabama when she'd come down for the business investment, they felt that Lawrence Brooks's daughter marrying an Alabama rancher was cause for an invasion.

And invade they did.

The Claremont Bed-and-Breakfast had been filled to capacity since the day they announced the wedding, not with wedding guests but with camera crews and news personnel. Television vans were parked on every corner and even at the end of the Cutter driveway.

Dana wrote a personal apology explaining how sorry she was that her presence had caused so many people to overtake Claremont, and she had Mary print it in the church's bulletin. But the tiny town's residents didn't mind. All the extra people only added to the number of shoppers in the square and boosted business for everyone.

So, on the day of the wedding, the entire town was

invited. Dana and John needed them, in a way, to form a privacy barrier. Because Dana wanted to get married in the place where she first visualized a wedding to the man she loved, at that section of the trail bordered by the vibrant purple, hot-pink and red rhododendrons.

In each guest's invitation, they'd included a dude ranch trail map, which specified the path to take for the wedding, a trail John had called "Dana's Wedding Trail."

Because it would have been impossible for everyone to gather at the spot where they would pledge their vows, the guests were instructed to border the path, from the beginning to the curve filled with rhododendrons, and the bride would pass through and therefore see everyone on her way to the groom.

Dana loved the idea, and she also loved the fact that with the townspeople lining the path and the woods forming a cool canopy overhead, the paparazzi couldn't invade the actual ceremony. They snapped as many photos as possible from their industrial-size cameras, and the helicopter hovering overhead got as close as it could, but there was no way that they would be there when Dana rounded that final curve, saw that stunning display of color—and the compelling rancher who'd held her heart since that first day she'd stepped on his farm.

Walking ahead of Dana, Abi tossed flower petals from a basket and said hello to her friends as she passed them on the path. And Ryan walked beside Dana to give her away.

She smiled, glanced at her brother, the guy who'd come so far over the past few weeks, seeing how much she'd fallen in love with Claremont and understanding how much she'd fallen in love with John.

"You ready, sis?" he asked softly, putting his hand on hers as he paused before handing her to her future husband.

Her heart swelled with admiration, with pride and with love. "I'm ready."

Ryan kissed her cheek, took her hand and put it in John's.

Brother Henry smiled and spoke of commitment and love and trials and endurance and children and family. Dana tried to listen to every word, but her vision focused so intently on John, on this man that she'd come to know so well, respect so deeply and love so completely, that the words all blurred together to create a memory.

"I've never been happier," John said softly.

"I haven't, either." She took a small step closer, eager to begin their lives as one. And they stood there, looking in each other's eyes and envisioning the wonderful future they'd share together.

Then Dana heard Ryan's chuckle. And then another snicker from the crowd. John glanced at the group and must have seen the same thing Dana saw, because several hands had moved to mouths to cover up their laughter.

"What—what is it?" Dana asked.

"Brother Henry said y'all can kiss," Abi announced. "But you're just standing there!"

Then they realized they'd missed a rather important

part of the ceremony, and John's deep dimples popped into place as he leaned around Dana and looked to Abi.

"I'm supposed to kiss her now?"

Abi, and everyone else who heard his question, yelled, "Yes!"

And, as soon as Dana stopped giggling, to her delight, he did.

* * * * *

If you enjoyed this story by Renee Andrews,
be sure to check out the other books this month
from Love Inspired!

Dear Reader,

My preacher, Wayne Dunaway (who Brother Henry is modeled after), often reminds our congregation to "Let go, and let God." I think we all go through times in our life when we try to handle life's problems and struggles on our own, only to realize that if we let go and turn the situation over to God, everything will work out fine.

I'm hoping, if you're facing struggles now, that *Heart of a Rancher* will remind you to let go, and let God. You can't go wrong if you do!

I enjoy mixing facts and fiction in my novels, and you'll learn about some of the truths hidden within the story on my website, www.reneeandrews.com. While you're there, you can also enter contests for cool prizes.

Additionally, my website includes alternate beginnings for some of my novels and deleted scenes that didn't make the final cut. If you have prayer requests, there's a place to let me know on my site. I will lift your request up to the Lord in prayer. I love to hear from readers, so please write to me at renee@reneeandrews.com.

Blessings in Christ,
Renee Andrews

Questions for Discussion

1. Dana begins her journey by wrecking her car, hitting a cow and then walking a mile in high heels. Have you ever had a day where everything seemed to go wrong from the start? How did that turn out for you?

2. A socialite on a small Alabama ranch is a prime example of a fish-out-of-water story. How did the Cutters make sure Dana felt welcome at their home?

3. Dana's father found God again on his deathbed. Have you known someone who has waited a lifetime before finding faith?

4. Have you or has someone you know reaffirmed faith due to the loss of a loved one?

5. The women gathered together to prepare meals for Mitch Gillespie. How does this action reflect the close-knit community of Claremont and the familial atmosphere of the Claremont Community Church?

6. Why do you think Dana's brother, Ryan, was so opposed to his sister assisting start-up businesses and inexperienced entrepreneurs? Do you think it all had to do with money?

7. Eden Sanders lived next door to her daughter's family. This is often still the case in the South, where families tend to settle down near each other and get together often. Is this the case where you live? Do you think this would be beneficial? Why or why not?

8. If people do not have family living close by, do you believe their church family should assume that role? Why or why not?

9. John wanted Dana to move to Alabama, marry him and live on the farm. However, he wasn't willing to live off her inheritance and wanted to "make it" on his own. What does this say about him?

10. John's dream to have a dude ranch in Alabama was rejected by the banks because it wasn't a typical venture, and because John didn't have experience in running a dude ranch. Have you ever had an idea that you believed would be successful, only to have it shot down by the powers that be because it wasn't traditional?

11. Do you think part of the appeal of Alabama to Dana was the chance to get out of the fishbowl of living in front of the paparazzi? Do you think that the paparazzi would leave them alone once they settled down in Alabama? Can you think of celebrities who have chosen to live outside the limelight? Was their attempt successful?

SPECIAL EXCERPT FROM

Love Inspired HISTORICAL

*With her own business in a fledgling frontier town,
Cassie Godfrey will be self-sufficient at last. But her
solitary plans are interrupted by four young orphans—
and one persistent cowboy.*

Read on for a sneak peek of
THE COWBOY'S UNEXPECTED FAMILY by Linda Ford.

"How long do you think it will take to contact the children's uncle?"

"I wouldn't venture a guess. Why? You already wishing I was gone?"

"You make me sound rude and ungrateful. I'm not. I just have plans. Goals. Don't you?"

Roper stared off in the distance for a moment, his expression uncharacteristically serious. Then he flashed Cassie a teasing grin. "Now that you mention it, I guess I don't. Apart from making sure the kids are safe."

"I find that hard to believe. Don't you want to get your own ranch?"

Roper shrugged, his smile never faltering. "Don't mind being free to go where I want, work for the man I wish to work for."

"Wouldn't you like to have a family of your own?"

"I never think of family. Never had any, except for the other kids in the orphanage." He laughed. "An odd sort of family, I guess. No roots. Changing with the seasons."

Cassie didn't know how to respond to his description of family. With no response coming to her mind, she shifted back to her concern. "Roper, about our arrangement. I—"

He chuckled. "I know what you're going to say, but this isn't about you or me. It's about the kids."

"So long as you remember that."

"I aim to. I got rules, you know. Like never stay where you're not wanted. Don't put down roots you'll likely have ripped out."

She guessed there was a story behind his last statement. Likely something he'd learned by bitter experience. "I plan to put down roots right here." She jabbed her finger toward the ground.

"That's the difference between you and me." The grin remained on his lips, but she noticed it didn't reach his eyes.

Whispers and giggles came from behind the wooden walls. "Do you think the children will be okay?"

"You did good in telling them they'll be safe here." His grin seemed to be both approving and teasing.

"They will be safe as much as it lies within me to make it so." And they'd never be made to feel like they were burdens. Not if Cassie had anything to do with it.

Don't miss THE COWBOY'S UNEXPECTED FAMILY by Linda Ford, the next book in the COWBOYS OF EDEN VALLEY *series, available March 2013 from Love Inspired Historical!*

To Trust or Not to Trust a Cowboy?

Former Dallas detective Jackson Stroud was set on moving to a new town for his dream job, until he makes a pit stop and discovers on the doorstep of a café an abandoned newborn and Shelby Grace, a waitress looking for a fresh start. He decides to help Shelby find the baby's mother, and through their quest he believes he's finally found a place to belong, while Shelby's convinced he will move on eventually. What will it take to convince Shelby that this is one cowboy she can count on?

Bundle of Joy

by

Annie Jones

Available March 2013!